Judges, Rulers and One Angry Levite

A Book of Historical Fiction that is built upon the Biblical Book of Judges

by

Gordon C. Krantz

COVER
The Angry Levite leaves Bethlehem
with his concubine and pack donkey.

Copyright © 2008
Gordon C. Krantz

Author contact: gnrkrantz@aol.com

Publisher: Lulu.com

ISBN   978-0-6151-8222-3

Contents

Section	Page
Introduction	1
Background	5
Othniel	9
Ehud	17
Shamgar	29
Deborah	41
Jael	45
Barak	49
Gideon	55
Abimelech	63
Tola	69
Jair	71
Jephthah	73
Ibzan	79
Elon	85
Abdon	89
Samson	03
The Mother	99
The Willing Young Levite	103
Micah	109
Abi-Dan	113
One Angry Levite	119

INTRODUCTION

All that we really know about these men and women, who mostly were judges and rulers in the time between the settlement of the Land by the Israelites after their Exodus and the time of Samuel, is what is recorded in the Book of Judges. The time span is probably from about 1400 BC (or even as late as 1250 BC) to 1050 BC; historians argue about the exact starting date.

Sometimes we are given well-developed histories in the Book of Judges, and sometimes the record is as sparse as a single sentence. A good example of the last is the story of Shamgar, about whom the Book only says, "After him (the previous judge) ruled Shamgar, who slew six hundred Philistines with an ox goad." And that's all. That sentence is what caused this book, because one night about 3 AM I lay awake wondering about Shamgar, and finally got up and started to imagine his story. The rest of the stories then began to unfold.

The stories in this present book are historical fiction. They are not an attempt to improve the Bible, but to give some sense of what a person had to think like in those circumstances in order to speak and act in the ways that are recorded.

I consider the stories in the Book of Judges in our English versions to be as accurate history as is possible when the originally inspired text is transmitted and translated. Sometimes fragmentary, always brief, but trustworthy. What I have added is fiction.

The stories here will not stand alone. To fully understand them, you have to read the original record, the Book of Judges. It is for this reason that the Bible reference is given at the head of each chapter. The stories may seem incomplete or obscure if you don't have the information that is given in the Bible, because sometimes the story here takes that information for granted.

Some of the stories continue to the death, or nearly to the death, of the narrator. A prime example is Samson, whose story is his thoughts just at the point of his final strong-man act. Other stories will leave you to imagine for yourself what transpires in the mind of the "hero" next. Jephthah is an example of that; the story ends while he still has six years to carry his burden of grief and guilt.

Some of the protagonists are judges. Some are merely rulers or leaders, and some are only walkers-on in the Bible. Contrary to what you might expect of the agents of the LORD, the judges are not an unbroken line of saintly people. Some were even mean-spirited. They were His instruments and they were human, and He used each for His purpose. Each had a part in shaping the nation of Israel prior to the days of David.

The final story is that of the Angry Levite. He is not named by the author of the Book of Judges. Though his story appears at the end of the Book of Judges, it is evident that the events took place soon after the Israelites entered the Land. He is neither a judge nor any kind of ruler. He is just one angry Levite.

In the time and place of the judges, life was different from the present. The narratives usually give no explanation of things that may appear strange or irrelevant to you. Examples are the beard of the smith and the birds painted on the jar in the story of Shamgar. So I have provided footnotes that give further explanation for some of these things. If you find something that is strange or unexplained in the text, there will usually be a footnote to flesh it out.

On the other hand, this is not a scholarly work. The text, as I said earlier, is fiction when it goes beyond the record of the Bible. The footnotes are not citations of the literature, no do I provide a bibliography that cites the authorities for what is in the text and footnotes. Serious scholars are not likely to find here anything that is new. Instead I have only tried to be faithful to the general understandings of historians of that period.

In this text I use the Name of the LORD, spelled with all capital letters. This is the practice in most modern Bible translations. The people of that day probably used the Name spelled (in all consonants, because Hebrew had no written vowels) as JHWH and probably pronounced as "Jahweh." In later centuries the Name became thought of as too holy to speak and so the name "Adonai," meaning "lord" was used when the Book was read. To help to remember this in nearly modern times the then-invented Hebrew vowel points of "Adonai" were written in above the JHWH and some translators read both the consonents of JHWH and the vowels of Adonai and thought that the Name was "Jehovah." It's too late to reverse the confusion, so in this book I will use LORD, to be distinguished from "lord" meaning a person to be respected or obeyed. And read the section that follows, labeled "Background." It will set the stage.

Background

The time period of the Judges is: from the time of the Israelite invasion of the Land under Joshua until just about the time of Samuel, the man who anointed first Saul and then David as kings over Israel. In terms of dates in the chronology that I prefer, this is from about 1400 BC or even 1250 BC to 1050 BC. The *rough* dates are:

```
2000 BC ......................................... Abraham
1500 BC .........................................Moses born
    1450 or 1250 BC ‹--- Judges ---› 1120 BC
1000 BC ............... Samuel, Kings Saul & David
 500 BC ............................................... Daniel
 1 BC/1 AD ............................Jesus Christ
 500 AD ........................................ King Arthur
1000 AD ..................................... Leif Erickson
1500 AD .........................Christopher Columbus
2000 AD .................................. You are here
```

We have some historical information about this period of time, but a lot of detail is missing from the record. I have written a small book of this history, "The Times of the Judges." It is available from the sam sources as this book.

The last half of the period was a time of chaos in the eastern Mediterranean lands, including the Land of Israel. A contemporaneous Egyptian record says that "the isles were in tumult." Egypt from the south, and the Hittite empire from the north, had fought each other to a standstill. Both empires were enfeebled, and there was a power vacuum.

There was extensive movement of peoples. The fall of Troy in far western Turkey as recorded in the "Iliad" appears to be part of this. The Hittite empire, in what now is eastern Turkey, fell and was not really replaced. The tumult finally reached the borders of Egypt in the south of Palestine. Egypt did not fall, but it was impotent in comparison to what it had been. It had previously ruled, or at least it was able to control, all of Palestine and half-way up the east coast of the Mediterranean Sea. Now its control reached only to south Palestine and a few bits along the coast.

There were assorted invasions onto the settled land in Syria and Palestine by what appear to be nomadic or at least mobile peoples and tribes. The records of the Egyptian foreign office contain the wails of city kings appealing for help, but no help came. Egypt could not or would not rescue its nominal outposts.

A mixed host, the "Sea Peoples," was surging along the Aegean Sea and Greece, the islands such as Cyprus, to the south Turkish coast, Syria, and Palestine. They were a tremendous historical force. Their wave finally broke on a desperate Egypt which just managed to hold them off. They worked along the seacoast and mostly settled there, eventually establishing formidable city states at places like Gaza and Ashdod and Gath.

The Sea Peoples were such groups as the Tjekker, the Denyen, the Sikel, the Weshesh and the Peleshti. (Sorry about the spellings, but the records in Egypt and elsewhere were not kept in English, so they have had to be translated. We have to guess on some of the sounds: Peleshti was spelled as "plst" in Egyptian, which like Old Hebrew doesn't have vowels. And our spoken consonants don't sound exactly like theirs. So don't complain when various English writers use different spellings.)

The group among the Sea Peoples whom we know most about is the plst or Peleshti, now spelled "Philistines." We know the most about them because the Jews wrote about them at length. Evidently the Jews considered all of the Sea Peoples to be Philistines. Who can blame them? The Sea Peoples were the Vikings of their day, raiding and occupying. Who cared whether they were from Norway or Sweden or Denmark? just as the English of 1000 AD called all the Vikings "Danes". It is true, of course, that other evidence clearly indicates that the Philistines were the most prominent among the Sea Peoples who settled in the Land.

As I said, the Middle East was in chaos. It was into this chaotic power vacuum that Joshua led the Children of Israel into Canaan. They were faced, not with an entrenched empire such as Egypt, but with a collection of Canaanite city states, which they attacked one by one. No imperial Egyptian troops opposed them.

And at first, no Sea Peoples. It was only after Israel had occupied the hill country of Palestine that they encountered the power of the Sea People. And the Israelites were not an empire, either. They were scattered tribes, owing allegiance to the LORD and to His Law rather than to a king. They were settling into the Land.

If you have read your Bible, you know the cycle: the Israelites became ensnared in the religions of the Canaanites, incorporating the gods and their ceremonies into their own practices. As God had warned, this led to the Israelites being given over to various oppressors, such as the nomadic raiders from the deserts to the east, the budding empires to the north, some unconquered Canaanite city kings - - and the Sea Peoples, whom they called Philistines.

Then God would raise up a "judge," a man or woman who would rally all or part of Israel back to the Law (usually) and would lead a struggle against the oppressors. There would be return to the Law (usually) and liberation. Then the same lapse into polytheism would return, the Israelites would corrupt their religion, and new oppressors would fall upon them.   And a new judge would be needed.

The resulting record that the Israelites left for us, the Book of Judges, is not a coherent history.   The judges are not given in chronological order, and some of them were contemporaneous with each other.   The book is a set of illustrations, and the theme of those illustrations is that cycle of apostasy-oppression-judgeship-reform-apostasy.

Oh yes, the plst or Peleshti or Philistines: one of their legacies is that in Roman times the Land became known by their name – Palestine.

OTHNIEL

Judges 1:11 - 15
Judges 3:7 - 11

Othniel was apparently the first judge, as well as the one whose story heads the Book of Judges.

Old Caleb[1] -- and I mean that title with all respect and affection -- Old Caleb was a man to follow. All my life, I have tried to live like he lived: a steadfast follower of the LORD, a man of long vision and strength, a man of wisdom and of generosity. Yes, I know that some of these things were not done in his own strength, but I have prayed for them for myself and I have tried my best to live them out.

Old Caleb, my uncle, was one of only two men who had left Egypt in the bloom of manhood and who lived to enter the Land. He was not the leader of all the host of our people -- Joshua, the other man who lived, was that -- but he was honored by all and he was respected. And he did great things.

Now, in my own old age, I find myself to be the one to whom all our tribes come for judgment. Old Caleb would be proud of his nephew. True, the most northerly tribes seldom consult me, but they live far away, three hard days' journey away, five days if you are not a solitary runner.

Old Caleb gave me my start. He had the faith to offer his daughter to the man who would take the city of Debir. I gathered my followers, with his blessing and urging, and the city fell to us. He gave me the wife who has stood by me all our lives together, a woman of wisdom and initiative, a credit to her father.

---

[1] Because Caleb was his uncle and his father-in-law, and because the exploits of Othniel himself are recorded in the conquest of Canaan, we know that Othniel was the first of the judges. After him, however, the order of judges is obscure.

And I? After I led the assault on the city I thought that my one big deed was finished and I settled down to the task of occupying my land and exploiting the upper and lower springs. Water in a dry land, thanks to my wife's thoughtfulness. That was going to be the end of adventures.

Then came the turbulent times of settlement, and they're still not over. We thought that we could just take over the land, and go about the peaceful business of farming and herding. But some of us -- why minimize it? most of us -- failed to do the thorough occupying that we were commanded to do, and the native peoples of the land raided back at us, and the peoples on the fringes of our territory raided as well. We had not rebuilt the city defenses, and furthermore we were not city people, and we lived in the open. We were being cut to pieces.

I knew why, and so did all the others who remembered the commandments of the LORD. Too many people took to the ways of the Canaanites. Maybe it was all right to dress like the people of the Land, and even to adopt their accent for our language. But the abomination was, and still is in places, that the people first allowed the Canaanites to continue their worship of the images, next they took the sons and daughters of the Canaanites into marriage and allowed them to bring in their idol worship. Finally, some of our people, maybe most of them, took part in the filth of the heathen worship. No wonder the LORD withheld His protection. We were being cut to pieces.

Cushan Rishathaim[2], Cushan the Doubly Wicked, a king from the far north in the Land of the Two Rivers[3],

---

[2] The name appears to mean something like "wicked double" in Hebrew.

[3] From his location in the north, we can assume that Cushan was of the people known in general as the Amorites but we are not given his nationality nor does history otherwise record him. The Two Rivers are the Euphrates and the Tigris, which extend from modern

extended his power southward until he reached all the way to our South Desert, the Negev. Yes, Egypt still though of our Land as their territory, but Egypt was impotent above the coastal plain. Cushan simply overpowered us in the hill country. Our people had to pay tribute to him, and his agents did what they wished and no one could oppose them. For eight years! until some of our people came to know that they had offended the LORD, the only LORD, by their abominations. Then we turned to the LORD and appealed to Him with our prayers and the prayers of the tribal leaders. Here in Debir we searched out those Levites[4] who had remained faithful to the LORD, and our cry went up to heaven.

This went on for some time. Then one day, while I was in my house praying, there came a Voice saying, "You are the one." I looked around, but there was no one there. My wife and sons were in the field. I thought, "I know that I'm the one. Before the LORD, each of us is to blame for bringing on the oppression of Cushan." But the Voice said again, "You are the one." At the same time, a feeling like I was going to burst grew within me, so that I staggered out of the door into the sunshine. Nothing had changed out there, but I still felt the growing Presence within me, and then I knew that I was called. Don't ask me how I knew, because I can't say. There are no words to express this Filling, this thrust[5]. And I knew that I had to rally our people against Cushan. I, who am mere leader of a small city.

It's one thing to know what you must accomplish. It's another thing to work out how to do it, and to follow through. What could we do, and how could we do it?

Turkey to southern Iraq.

[4] The Levites were the Israelite tribe from which were drawn the priests and who were especially separated to serve the LORD..

[5] Usually in the Book of Judges we are not told just how the LORD spoke to people.

But somehow the thoughts came to me, and I could see what to do, at least the first steps.

First, I took my usual early seat in the city gates, and waited until only those few of the other elders whom I could absolutely trust had joined me. Then I told them, loud enough for any agents listening to hear, "Come out with me to my fields. I want to show you something." We went. My fields could be seen from the gates, so I knew that other elders who came to the gate later would see us. I bent down, then sat, and asked the others to sit as though we were looking at something. I swore them to secrecy, and we discussed what we could do to rid ourselves of Cushan.

His agents among us were known, of course, and we hadn't dared do anything about them. So they were our first concern. Then came the concern about how to mobilize our people for a revolt. We decided to start by taking the other local elders whom we could trust, those who worshiped the LORD, into our plans. Because we worked with those who worshiped the LORD, we could protect our secrets by an oath.

It took a month before I could persuade the other elders here in the Negev that we should and could rise up. It took another six months to work throughout the Land, first persuading and then steeling the resolve to face the great foreign power of Aram Between the Rivers. And we had to do it without alerting the agents of Cushan. If we were to succeed, we had to strike suddenly and unexpectedly. We, and later the cells that spread throughout the Land, would meet to pray and to renew oaths of silence and unity, and to work out the plan of attack. The Levites, who could travel without attracting notice[6], were our best leaven.

---

[6] We have some evidence that Levites were more mobile than other Israelites.

I heard that one of Cushan's agents in a tribe north of here got knowledge that something was afoot. He was soon found in a wadi[7] with his neck broken by a fall. I didn't ask anything about it. There was no need to call Cushan's attention to it.

On the arranged day, just after harvest, our leaders throughout the land struck at the agents of Cushan. We had to be especially thorough in the north, and then we were able to pick off any surviving agents in the south before they could break through to their master.

The next day, starting here in the Negev, we set in motion a rolling wave of men who, with whatever arms they could find, moved north. In the six days it took to reach Laish in the north, the men in the northern areas had to go about their business normally in order to keep military silence until the rest of us reached them. As it turned out, our caution was unnecessary after we got started.

On the fifth day, our full force converged from the highlands east and west of Laish[8], and we assembled there. We used the plain of Laish to gather our troops. The High Priest himself had come out of the Jordan slopes, and he led us in an appeal to the LORD for victory. I had organized the men into companies of hundreds and thousands. We were so many that we had to have Levites stationed in our midst to relay the words of the High Priest.

We all took the oath that we would turn from the abominations of the Canaanites when we returned home. From what happened in later years, I think that some men had their fingers crossed behind them.

---

[7] A gully or ravine in the Middle East is usually called a wadi.

[8] This is the town that was later renamed Dan - - see the story in this book of The Willing Young Levite.

It seemed like a let-down next day when we marched into the home territory of Cushan. There was no opposition to speak of. Cities are few in that region except for Damascus farther north, and other than the imperial runners and pack animals on the trade routes, there is not much travel. We knew that the runners had set off when we were first spotted, but Cushan's forces just melted away before us. The LORD had heard our prayer. After marching a full day into the area that was not our Land, we stopped and waited.

Another three days, and a herald came to us under a flag of truce. His speech was coarse and foreign, but his message was clear enough. Cushan was busy with problems elsewhere, and did not intend to contest the Land with us at this time[9]. We thanked the herald, gave him provisions for his return, and turned ourselves toward home. Our human carpet unrolled in reverse order. My men and I reached Debir only three weeks after we had left home.

My wife prepared supper, and I went to bed. Once again I thought that this one act would be the end of it, even though the Presence still could be felt within me. No, I can't tell you how it feels. But it now felt steady and restful, not urgent and thrusting like it was at the first. I was ready to settle into Debir and my adjoining fields, with their upper and lower springs, and be the leader of a little city.

It was not to be. Leading the wave of men north had made me conspicuous, and everyone knew who it was that had formed the revolutionary cells and worked out the plan. They may not have known the power of the LORD behind it, and perhaps they saw only a man.

---

[9] The Book of Judges says that Othniel overcame Cushan, but doesn't give any details. There may not have been a battle at all.

That was many years ago. Old Caleb is long gone. In fact, he died before the days of Cushan the Doubly Wicked. The wife of my youth, my strong helper and counselor, is gone now. My sons have sons, and one has a grandson. Much of my work has been undone by the backsliders who have gone back to the abominations of the Canaanites.

The people call me a judge. Before all this happened, I didn't know what a judge could be. What has happened is that first locally, and then from as far north as the Lake of Fresh Water[10] and beyond, men with problems and disputes have come to me for advice or decision. If it were not for the Presence, I could not have faced these problems. Even so, they do bear heavily on me.

I have to decide: should this man's debt of a measure of barley be forgiven because his creditor, against the Law, held his cloak for security overnight? This man, who is claimed to have visited a Canaanite prostitute in the Baal temple - - did he do it? If so, what should be the penalty? Are there credible witnesses? This man has gone to a city of refuge, claiming that he killed by accident -- are there witnesses who can establish that he in fact lay in wait or had indicated hatred against his victim beforehand? I have to convene the elders of the city and cast the final vote, or at least argue the disposition. This sheep that has strayed -- did the finder try to locate the owner? What shall be done to this man who was seen taking part in the celebration of the Asherah[11], and who now swears allegiance to the LORD? All these weigh heavily upon me. What if I fail to judge aright?

---

[10] The Lake of Fresh Water is the Galilee.

[11] The Asherah was a pagan religious person and/or his/her cult object, usually a pole or an upright stone.

I have had to travel to other tribal areas sometimes, persuading or admonishing until right is done. I don't do that any more. I am old. Soon I will go to be with my fathers. When I do, I want to go knowing that Old Caleb would be proud of me.

EHUD

Judges 3:12 - 30

Ehud would have had to be crafty to accomplish what he did.

They should have suspected me. Even though I spent three years preparing the opportunity, they should have known that a lot of us Benjamites are left-handed[12]. But they're Moabites.

It was gradual, until they took Jericho. Until then, the Moabites had just drifted into the Land from the east, and the Amalekites from the south were already mixed in with our people in the South Desert, the Negev. Then when the king of Moab -- I don't regret for a minute what I did to King Eglon! -- joined forces with the Ammonites to his north, they openly took Jericho. The loss of the City of Palms itself was of no account to us, because our people didn't actually live in that cursed place. But its great spring of fresh water was an important resource to us, and its loss was what woke us up[13].

But we couldn't do much about it. Moab was an organized kingdom, supported by the tribal people of Ammon and Amelek, the ones who did much of the actual oppression. We could rise up in a local area and even free a city from the oppressors, but it didn't last. Moab would put together a small military force and take it back, killing and enslaving too many of us to make rebellion worth while.

Eighteen years of occupation by Moab. I was a young lad when it began, so I had no real memory of when we were free. My father would tell me stories of when the

---

[12] The Bible comments on that. See I Chron 12:2, Judges 20:16.

[13] After the destruction of Jericho under Joshua, the Israelites did not re-occupy the city. But they could not have ignored the great spring of fresh water in this dry land, the spring which had been the cause of Jericho's being built in the first place. The loss of this agricultural resource would be a just cause for war.

Land was first taken from the heathen. We lived then very much like we live now, most of us in those little unfortified farming villages. But we were rich. We could keep all that we could raise. There was no tax to Moab then, only the small LORD's portion which was due to the Levites and the Sanctuary.

Eglon, when he established his power in the Land, put taxation on an organized basis. He with his army to enforce his tax took a full third of our produce, and when the Ammorites[14] and Amalekites saw something beyond that which they wanted, they took that too. Eglon organized even us, demanding that the work of tax collecting be done by the heads of our families and the elders of our cities.

It was bad enough here in Benjamin, but the Judah tribe south of us, in the dry and stony Negev, had a double burden. Their land produced poorly, so they had a harder time living on the portion that was legally left to them. And the Amalekites, who were herdsmen like the Judahites, helped themselves to the remaining flocks of Judah. When the people of Judah complained to Eglon, he laughed and said something like, "Boys will be boys." We had the oppression of a king, but not his protection.

The Moabites brought with them their abomination, Chemosh. The idols of the local Canaanites are morally worse than Chemosh, but the god of Moab is a warlike god. In the name of Chemosh, Eglon claimed all the Land to be his, though he actually occupied only the territory of Benjamin and Judah, with its enclosed territory of Simeon, and the southern part of Ephraim. Eglon set up a temple to Chemosh in the City of Palms, and settled a garrison there. We were treated as occupied, in the Land that was by right our own Land, given to us by the LORD.

---

[14] Ammonites, Amalekites, and other "ites" were a continual thorn in the side of Israel for the next several hundred years.

Over time our burden of taxation became worse. If a family or clan failed to deliver the tribute to Eglon on time, he sent a detachment of troops and they took everything they could find. They even enslaved some of our people to be servants and laborers in Moab. The result was that we were forced to organize ourselves, first for the effective collection of tax. As we did that, we found that we could organize for other purposes as well. Early on, we used our organization, based on the system of heads of families as Moses (blessed be his memory) had set it up many years ago, to establish a system of communication among ourselves. Though we didn't dare to say much about rebellion for fear of informers among us, we all knew that we could act together if the chance came.

As I became a man, I found that gradually my responsibilities enlarged. From being the head of a family, I became the head of my clan. Eventually, I became the one in charge of assembling the taxes from both Benjamin and Judah and leading the tribute caravan to Eglon's palace in Moab. Eglon would move his court to the western border, just across the Jordan from Jericho, to receive the tribute caravan. Oh, Eglon was a greedy man! He wanted to see and touch the tribute personally.

For three years, I brought the tribute and delivered it to Eglon. I saw how much whispering and intrigue went on in his court, with different officials trying to gain his favor. I noticed that he liked to be given little gifts, even though he could take whatever he wanted. His hangers-on would come up and whisper to him, or take him aside, and slip little things into his hand. He was a collector, and he liked to add to his store of Egyptian seals and scarabs. He even had his best collection brought to his Jordan seasonal headquarters for receiving tribute, and he displayed it in his throne room. We saw it.

In that first year that I brought the tribute, I realized that I could conceal my left-handedness. I didn't know why at the time, it just seemed to be a good idea to keep something back. So I shifted to right-handedness. It isn't as hard as it looks, because we left-handers have to be good with both hands if we're going to use the things of this world that are made for right-handers. Of course, when I got home I reverted to my natural handedness. But in Eglon's court, I was right-handed. Fortunately, I didn't have to write. The Moabites didn't realize how literate we of the People are, and they thought we were just crude farmers. I took my receipts, bowed to the king, and didn't even look at the tablets in his presence. Of course I could read them[15]. The writing of Moab is almost the same as the Lip of Canaan.

It was hard to hold my stomach in Eglon's court, what with all those statues and inscriptions to Chemosh. To make it worse, Eglon had set up boundary stones all along his border, statues of Chemosh, each with a little Eglon standing before it. When we crossed the Jordan with the tribute, we had to pass a big Chemosh statue. I didn't look at it any more than I had to. It was an abomination.

By the time of the third tribute caravan I led, I had bought an Egyptian scarab seal that one of our men had found in the ruins of a small city. When I delivered the tribute, I bowed to Eglon and told him that I had a present for him[16] . He let me go up to his throne and hand him the scarab, and he even smiled. He said that he would

---

[15] The alphabet had been invented, and there was a writing system we call "Paleo-Hebrew." An alphabet enables almost anyone to quickly learn how to read and write. That many Israelites were literate is indicated by the fact that Gideon was able to catch a young man at random (Judges 8:14) and make him write down names.

[16] The start of Ehud's campaign to get close to Eglon. Without this careful and gradual approach, no king of those days or later would let a foreigner get within striking range.

remember me, and that was what I had counted on. It was necessary for me to have his trust, even though I didn't have my plan fully worked out at that time.

The third year, I again brought him a scarab as a gift. This time, I had searched among the families for an especially good one. It was cut in a green stone, and had a silver clasp. I had to pay well for it. I couldn't yet tell anyone of the plan that was taking shape in my mind. I wasn't well thought of in some circles, because I had been going to that heathen court. Some people thought that I had gone over to Eglon's side, for that matter. But those who had gone with me on the tribute caravans stuck up for me. They knew me.

I told you that I was the leader of the tribute caravan. More than that, I had been authorized by the King of Moab to head up the bureaucracy of our people. No, he didn't give me instructions personally. He had court officials for that. My tax job made me a sort of deputy king. I worked hard at making the job not only tolerable to our tribes, but even appreciated. I set up a system of linkages among the elders of the families, so that we could work together on such simple things as clearing the paths between the villages to make travel easier. I took care to not give my tribe and family any special favors in this, and I thought that I had at least grudging acceptance among the people.

Anyhow, when I got to the court that fourth year, after the tribute had been tallied in front of Eglon, he looked at me with a smirk. It was plain that he expected another present, so I said to him, "Great King, I have a 'message' for you, but I don't want to give it here in the open court. It's rather special. Can I see you more privately?" The king's eyes glittered -- did I tell you that he was a greedy man? -- and he said, "Come to my roof chamber later. I'll call for you."

In a short while, even before we had to endure the humiliation of eating and drinking in the king's unclean hall, a guard came for me.

Eglon was in his roof chamber, a closed room not at all like our open summer roof sleeping places. Closed in, it smelled. The king told his guards to wait outside the door[17], and turned to me. I said, "Great King, this is an unworthy token of our devotion to you. It was found by our people, and I hope that it will please you. We don't know what it is, but I've noticed that you collect these things." I didn't tell him that I knew that the seal bore the cartouche of Thutmose III, the great king of Egypt just before our time.

Well, Eglon took the scarab and turned it over. He said, "You've done well. I like you. Next year, when you bring the tribute, see if you can find some more of these." I bowed my way out, noting that the door to the chamber was fastened by one of those locks that can be closed and opened from the inside, and can be locked from the outside by reaching into the hole and dropping the tumblers, but can only be opened from the outside by one of those big keys. And the key was stored behind the door. If the Lord was kind to me, it would be the same next year. Now my plan was clear, and I knew what I had to do.

Our caravan passed back over the ford of the Jordan. The Moabite guard squad that had been detailed to us dropped out, as usual, at the boundary stone of Chemosh.

That year, at home, I prepared. I couldn't tell anyone just what I intended to do, not even my wife. I told her that the big knife was for protecting the caravan.

Bronze is easy to work. I used an old Canaanite sword, cutting it to a cubit's length and chiseling off the guard.

---

[17] Just about the ultimate indication of Eglon's trust of Ehud.

The handle was already good enough, though I had to chisel off the disk at its end. Heating the end to anneal it, I hammered a new point on it, work-hardening the point and the edges before honing it sharp. I made the sheath from goatskin, with some hair on it to soften the bundle in case I was patted down. Then I made straps to bind it inside my right thigh, checking to see that it was concealed by my tunic and its kilt. The fringe was, as is customary, on the left[18], so that I could reach in for the knife easily. I had made the knife as long as could be concealed. Eglon was a very fat man, and I wanted to be sure to reach his life. Then I was ready.

The caravan of tribute was made up. I asked for, and received, many extra men to go with me. Getting them was not difficult, since they would have the adventure of visiting a royal court. I asked that all of them be armed, because the caravan was valuable, and I made up a rumor that the Amorites might raid us. Before we reached the Jordan, I sounded out each of the men, making sure that every one of them was loyal to his tribe. I hinted that this might be the last time we had to make the trip. No one got suspicious, because we had often wished that we didn't have to grovel before Eglon and they thought that I was just talking.

Our men concealed our weapons in a gully and crossed the Jordan and passed the Chemosh stone. That same day, we stood in Eglon's court and delivered the tribute.

Eglon, as before, was expecting something from me. After the delivery of the tribute, I bowed before him and said, "Great King, let me lead my men back across the river, and then I will return with something special." Greedy as ever, Eglon said, "Send them home in peace, and return and attend me in the roof chamber. May Chemosh go with them!"

---

[18] This kind of kilt is shown on Egyptian art of nearly that period showing men from Palestine.

So, when my men were safely past the boundary stone and out of earshot of the Moabite guards, I told them to make ready for a fast retreat. I was going, I told them, on a dangerous errand. If I did not return by sunset, they were to split up and scatter to their homes. Otherwise I would return and give them great news. They were to move back from the River for as long as it would take me to go and return.

Then I went back to Eglon. He had told the palace guards to expect me, and I was taken to the roof chamber.

I bowed and said, "Great King, I have a secret message for you." He turned to the guards and said, "Everyone leave us. Go down off the roof and wait for me to call you."

When all the guards were out of the immediate area, I approached the king and reached into my kilt with my left hand while reaching into my belt pouch with my right. The king watched my right hand, eager to see what novelty I had brought him. He didn't even notice the knife in my left hand until it entered his body, just below the breastbone. I said, "I have a message from the Lord for you," and I angled the knife upward and pushed.

Eglon's eyes bulged out and he grunted. He opened his mouth to scream, and I put my palm against the end of the knife handle and slammed it in as far as I could. The knife went in and the fat closed over it. Eglon slid out of the chair and lay still.

I kicked him to see if he could respond, but he was dead. So I went to the door, made sure that the key was inside, and closed the door. Then I reached into the hole and pushed the tumblers of the lock into place, took a deep breath, and walked out past the guards. If there was a second key, it would take the guards some time to find it, and I could not afford to hurry and raise suspicions. But the LORD was with me.

I reached the Jordan and crossed the ford. My men came out of the gullies where they had been waiting. I told them what I had done, and made it clear to them that now we would have to win our freedom from Moab or die. We had only a short time before the troops of Eglon would be after us.

I split our company into three. I delegated our bravest man, Joel, to lead the group that would fall upon the small Moabite garrison at the City of Palms. I personally commanded the group that would hold the fords of the Jordan. The one-third who appeared least brave were sent with messages to all the elders of the Ephraim. I made them learn the message by heart, and told them to run. I sent one man to alert the elders of Judah and Benjamin, using our system of communication.

Then we waited[19]. Nothing happened for a full day. I realized then the weakness of a nation that has a king. When the king was dead, no one ruled. The few who could aspire to the kingdom were faced first with the need to eliminate the king's legitimate heirs, who were back at the real palace. Then the claimants to the throne had to fight to see who would be the next king. We have no king. We have the LORD.

Men poured out of Ephraim, Benjamin, and Judah. Before the Moabites could rally a troop, we had command of the fords of the Jordan. The men who had come to us had been instructed to kill out any Amalekites and Ammorites they met, and they reported that the Judahites were pushing Amalek southward all

---

[19] How could Ehud have had time to rally the Israelites to attack Moab? The answer I've exploited here is that kingly succession in those days was messy and time-consuming when there were claimants to a suddenly-vacant throne. You had to literally kill the competition.

along the Negev. Any Ammorites who tried to cross east over the Jordan were cut down. Many of the Amalekites escaped by way of the Salt Sea[20], going around its south end to reach home.

Moab was out of commission as a nation. Its army was divided among those who claimed the throne, and the whole country was disorganized. When we scouted and realized what the situation was, we formed up our own troops by families and clans and invaded Moab. It was surprisingly easy. The common people had no stake in the family of Eglon, and they feared the army leaders who were contending for the throne. It was a great month. We lived off the land, treating the common people with as much respect as we could, for all that they worshipped an abomination, Chemosh. We had no such respect for the officials. We destroyed all the Chemosh images that we found, and before we were half way through the country, the leaders of the Moabite families came to us and asked for peace. We were glad to give it, on condition that our eighteen years of tribute be made up to us, and we returned to our Land with hostages from the leading families.

Then we had peace and freedom from occupation and taxation.

We have had peace with Moab ever since, and now I am old. I am still the leader of our tribes, but this time it is by their choice, because they have made me judge. I hear their troubles and give my advice, and they take it as command. I have been careful to shape my advice by the Law, and there are two Levites who attend me in rotation, whom I consult[21] before making a judgment. I recruit the Levites from the villages of all three tribes, rotating them to avoid favoritism.

---

[20] The Salt Sea is now called the Dead Sea.

[21] What better use for the Levites scattered throughout Israel? They should be the tribe most familiar with the Law of Moses.

Moab still pays tribute, and I see to its distribution. I try to be completely fair in this, and have had no serious complaints.

I will go to my fathers in peace.

Shamgar
Judges 3:31

Shamgar is the cause of this set of stories. I was musing at 3 AM about this man, who rates only one verse in the Bible, and the story came to me.

"It will cost you a pim[22] of good bronze, you know. Do you have that much?" The smith hefted the stubby pim weight in his hand as he looked me over.

The smith spoke the language with an accent, putting too much stress on the first part of each word, a bit jerky and without the smooth flow of sounds that we and the native people of the land use. Not that our own people are all free of accents; a couple of years ago a man from the Ephraim tribe came through from across the Jordan, trading, and he kept calling me "Samgar," as though he couldn't say "Shamgar.[23]"

This foreigner didn't look like the native people of the plain, and he didn't look like our people either. He was too tall, with strange light-colored hair cut short, and with a short light brown beard that left his upper lip bare[24]. All the foreign men do that to their beards even after being settled here for more than a generation. I didn't like the way he looked at me. I never liked the way the city people looked at me, and I wouldn't have come down here to the plain among them if I didn't have to. The

---

[22] There were no coins in those days. "Money" was so much weight in metal or goods. The pim was a unit of weight, and scale weights labeled "pim" have been found by archaeologists.

[23] As an Epraimite, he probably couldn't say "shibboleth" either - - see Judges 12:6.

[24] The Philistines were one of the several Sea Peoples who had invaded the Middle East. They seem, on several lines of evidence, to have come from the Aegean area, so I have given the smith a beard like those depicted by and of the contemporary Greeks. It would have seemed strange to an Israelite, who wore a full beard. The Israelites knew that the Egyptians shaved themselves all over, so shaving itself was not surprising.

townspeople of the plain all avoid us, but these newcomers are even worse. I've had some of them edge around to the windward side when we talked, trying not to show that they didn't like our smell. Sometimes they even say so. It is said of the foreigners that they get into a big basin of water almost every day and get rubbed and scraped and oiled. Who can afford that much water? Down here on the plain, maybe they can.

Anyhow, there is always this barely-concealed contempt for us. It sets my teeth on edge.

I looked down at the worn tip of my ox goad[25]. If I could afford to have that fixed, too --- But I was here to have the iron point of my plowshare restored[26]. You can't use bronze, much less the naked wood, for a plowshare. Iron is the only thing that lasts more than a day among the rocks, and my plowshare was blunted beyond usefulness. And since we in the hill country had no smiths -- it was because of these newcomers that we were forbidden to have them! -- I needs must go to this man who plainly showed that he thought that we farmers of the hill country were inferior.

The smith needed my answer. I suppose he didn't think that someone dressed like me would have good bronze.

"Yes, I have that much." He couldn't know what my plow had turned up on my land, a small wedge of silver that the former owner had either hidden of dropped or simply lost when my fathers invaded. We in the hills seldom see silver. I wasn't even sure how much it was worth in bronze.

---

[25] The goad was a pole with a point used to goad or prick the ox to make it keep going.

[26] The Philistines had a monopoly on this new metal, iron, and they wouldn't let Israelites do any ironwork. They had the military power to enforce their ban.

Well, it was time to do business. I dipped a hand into my pouch and produced the little wedge. I had rubbed the dirt and tarnish off it, and it winked in the sunlight. The smith's eyes lighted. His manner changed a bit, and I was suddenly more than a dirty farmer. If we had been alone I wouldn't have dared to trust him with my silver, but here in the edge of the city I knew that I could count on the elders to protect me that much. A bad reputation for the city would cost them more business than the wedge was worth.

The smith took the wedge and tossed it lightly in his palm. Then he took it over to the broken-off bottom half of a large jar that stood by his bench, filled with water. How strange these foreigners are! The jar actually had images painted on it, black sketches of some kind of bird with its head turned backward over its back[27]. The foreigners have brought in the fashion of painting pottery, and they all seem to like to paint birds with their heads turned back.

The smith dipped the wedge of silver in the water and rubbed it. Didn't he think it was clean enough? Ah, he was trying to see if it had enough dirt embedded in its crevices to affect the weight! Thrifty sort. And he didn't flinch when he touched the water that was made unclean by those images -- forbidden to us by the Law!-- on the jar.

He put the silver on one pan of the scale and the pim weight on the other. They just about balanced. The smith seemed reluctant to hand back the silver. Not that I was anxious to touch it, either, after it had been in that pagan jar.

---

[27] The pot with its painted birds is diagnostic of Philistine pottery. If you are shown such a pot fragment, you will know immediately that it is either Philistine or Greek of the same historical period.

I could see that the smith wanted the silver. It must have been of very good quality, but I was so unfamiliar with the metal that I couldn't judge.

"I could just clip off a small part of this wedge and credit you with a pim's worth of good bronze," the smith said, "but that small part wouldn't be worth as much to me because it would be too small to make anything. Is there something else I could do for you?"

My ox goad had served as my staff, even though it stood nearly a cubit over my head. We both looked at the worn bronze point. "Even reshaping and sharpening the goad wouldn't be enough, and I don't need anything else," I said.

The smith rolled the wedge in his hand. Then he spoke.

"Look, I like you. I've worked with enough of you hill country barbari -- farmers -- to be more comfortable with you than my fellow countrymen are. You act like a responsible man. And I want this silver for something I don't want to bother you about." He meant, no doubt, that it would have something to do with his religion. His religion! They worshipped an idol that was half fish, I'd heard. Well, I couldn't control that. "Tell you what. I'll sharpen your plow, and I'll replace that goad tip with a small tip of real iron. And I'll make a blade for the other end of the goad that you can use to clean the plowshare as you work[28]. I've made them before, and they're real handy. And for you I'll make it of standard bronze, and make the blade stand out to the side, so you can scrape the clay off the share without taking your hands off the plow handle.. You won't be able to use the goad as a staff any more, but you'll have the best ox goad in the hills."

---

[28] Many ox goads of that period had scrapers on the back end, but I don't know of any with the style described here.

It was getting late. I didn't want to spend the night in that town with whatever abominations they practice. It was time to come to a bargain. And really, what he offered was all that I wanted anyway.

"Done!" I said. "I'll leave these things with you and come back in two days. I'll trust you to do good work." The smith smiled -- they could smile, then! -- and actually held out his hand for a handshake. I couldn't refuse, though I rubbed my hand with clean sand after I was out of sight.

Two days later, I found that the smith was as good as his word. The plowshare was bright and sharp. And the goad, though a little heavier with the scraper blade on the back end, balanced much better. The iron tip of the goad was the best I'd seen.

The smith smiled again. "I thought I'd make the scraper blade on the goad extend a good hand span to the side," he said, "so I had to make it a little thinner than I had intended. But I've ribbed the back of it for strength." I wasn't used to having these foreigners smile at me, and being unsure of myself and not knowing what else to do, I just held out my hand. And he took it and even clasped my forearm with his left hand as we parted.

I was eager to get back to my farm. There was ferment in the air. You could almost hear it rumble through the hills. There had always been bad blood between our people in the hills and the native people and the foreigners of the plain and seashore. The native people resented having lost their land in the hill country when our forefathers swept in from across the Jordan, even though the hill land is stony and scrub-forested and infertile compared with the land in the plains.

The foreigners, sea people[29] who had not been gentle when they moved in on the natives of the plain and the

---

[29] Though the Sea People comprised Philistines, Sikel, Tjerker, and

22

seashore and took over their land, were just aggressive to everyone. They had brought in the use of iron, now cheap enough so that it was no longer used as rare jewelry, and they kept the working of iron as a monopoly. Especially they kept iron working away from our people in the hills, afraid that we would use iron to continue our conquest of the land. So they sent inspectors into the hills, sometimes guarded by their bronze-clad, iron-weaponed soldiers, to make sure that we didn't set up iron forges. We weren't allowed even to sharpen our own plowshares. Which is why I had to go to their smith.

We could live without the working of iron. What we couldn't live with was the taxation and the raids. Because the foreigners were strong and based themselves in their five fortified cities, we were no match for them militarily. They took as much of our crops in taxation as they wished, and then the stole from the little grain hoards that we were legally permitted to keep. It had become dangerous to store grain in any quantity where it might be found.

Finally, just a moon ago, there had been a clash between a group of our farmers and the foreigners, and a foreign soldier had been killed. There was rumor of an expedition from the foreigner's city to punish us, and our farmers were sending messengers to and fro with rumors and threats. With all this going on, I still had to go to get my plow sharpened, and had the good fortune to find a smith who was at least civil to me.

When I got home, my wife was waiting with a message. "It's true," she said, "our scouts have seen troops gathering into the city." (I had seen them too, and the news was not news to me.) "The word is that they'll send a big expedition against us. They can't bring their chariots into the hill country, but they look like they want to cut right through here to their settlement at Beth Shean[30]. They'll take everything, burn everything. What

others. But Shamgar probably called them all Philistines.

will we do with our cow? the ox? our few sheep? Shall I get everything ready to escape to our cousin to the east?"

"Wait," I said to her, "we can't just run away from a rumor." And that was where matters stood for at least a week. The messengers kept going among the families and clans.

Then word came that the foreigners had moved out of the city and were putting their chariots and troops in order for the march. For now, they were just drilling their men and getting the town people they had levied into shape, but in another few days they would be among us. The message came that we who wanted to defend our homes should gather in the foothills opposite the city, bringing three days' provisions, a water skin, and whatever weapons we had. Naturally, I went, taking my only "weapon," the ox goad.

Well, since I was so near to the assembly point, I got there in time to see the foreigners arrive for their assault. The charioteers took the horses to the rear, and the rest set up camp to get ready. You could tell that they knew we were gathering by the way they set up their camp, with the most impressive, shining-armored men getting out of the chariots and stationing themselves near the front, their red-crowned helmets[31] glowing in the afternoon sun. Then they set up in the very front one of those big body-sheltering shields they used to use[32],

---

[30] Egypt had settled Philistines as a garrison in the fortress of Beth Shean southwest of the Galilee and elsewhere in the Land such as in Gibeon.

[31] Contemporary Egyptian art shows Philistines wearing helmets with a circling crown of fiber or feathers colored red.

[32] The "figure eight" shield of the Aegean people had gone out of style by then, but it was recent enough and storied enough to be a sort of talisman, as I have made it here.

with their man-fish god[33] painted on it. The sun glinted off their armor and off the honed edges of their spears. They would advance into the hills tomorrow, we knew.

The sun set behind them, and we clustered behind the first foothills. More of our men were coming out of the hills, but we were still only a couple hundred. Our scouts had counted the host of the enemy. They were at least a thousand, counting the town levies of common people, with maybe seven hundred of the elite professional soldiers in their front ranks.

We sent men to scatter over a wide front behind the first row of hills to build fires, so that the enemy would see the smoke and the glow and think that we were a large army. We knew that, in the kind of fight ahead of us, against men who were famous as boasters, a show of force would help us.

Our elders gathered to discuss what to do in the morning. That would be the only time we could strike, with the eastern sun behind us and with the momentum of a downhill charge.

But when morning came, and we drew up in a line on the slope above the enemy, none of us wanted to make the next move. The enemy were already awake, getting ready to march into the hills, and the elite warriors had already slung their shields on their backs and stationed themselves in the front. They were used to fighting on foot[34], they with their chariots had gotten to their campsite before the foot soldiers had arrived yesterday, and they were in fine spirits. They were yelling at each other, and when they saw us, they yelled at us. And

[33] The prominent Philistine god was Dagon, half man and half fish, whom they had adopted from peoples farther east.

[34] Though the Egyptians and Hittites fought from aboard their chariots, ancient Greeks and probably Philistines used the chariot to get to the battle field and then dismounted to fight.

they began their usual boasting and their ridiculing of us at the tops of their great voices. Those who remembered the language of their fathers used it to chant some kind of poetry[35].

Then there was a shoving match in the front ranks, and out of it stood a big, broad warrior. He stamped and yelled and twirled his spear above his head, and he advanced to the open ground in front of the shield that bore the image of their god. The rest of the host quieted somewhat in order to hear his boasts and insults[36].

"Slaves!" he yelled at us. "Peasants! Stinking farmers! Louse factories! Unwashed barbarians! Behold us, the conquerors of all seacoasts! We will slaughter you and carry off your wives and daughters to spin our wool and carry our water, and to warm our beds!"

We all stood in silence. We don't do that sort of thing, to yell and curse with no dignity. How could we answer such unseemly racket? But we were angry, cold angry. They still outnumbered us and we had no iron weapons. Some of us had hoes and knives, some few had axes, the rest had whatever would serve as a club. Most of us had our little hooked vinedressing knives. I had my ox goad. And we were angry, and afraid and desperate.

"Vermin!" the man yelled, "Worshipers of a god you can't even see! Where is the LORD you call on!"

I don't know just what happened then, except that he had invoked the Name, and I felt the presence of a great Hand lifting me up and propelling me forward. I broke from our line and ran down the hill at the man who had

---

[35] The poetry would be epics of their conquests, probably the beginnings of epics like the Iliad and Odyssey, the works of Homer that were being founded at that time.

[36] Another legacy of the Philistine's probable Aegean origin. See the Greek heroes at Troy, and Goliath.

defiled what could not be defiled and had said what cannot be endured.

A red veil of rage was before my eyes, but strangely I could see clearly, and I was pushed at a speed I didn't know I possessed. The foreigner was standing with his mouth open, in the middle of a curse. Then he fumbled for the strap of his shield and swung it half way round to the front. He was bringing his spear into throwing position when I reached him, and he was not ready.

Without thinking, I spun my ox goad around and hooked the scraper blade behind his left knee[37]. I can see it now, the blade catching him just above the top strap of the greave that armored his shin. Then I jerked the goad back and pushed it forward to free it, but it was trapped and broke nearly half-way and I was left with maybe four cubits of shaft with its iron tip.

The big man crumbled and fell on his back. His arms flung out, the shield banging on the ground on one side and the spear falling out of his hand on the other. He was going to get up, so I spun the goad around again and drove the point between the scales of his chest armor. And he lay still.

There was dead silence for a moment. I had time to turn around and see our men standing as frozen as were the enemy ranks. I took a deep breath.

"For the LORD!" I screamed, and shook the goad over my head. There was a roar from our men, and they poured down the slope and had nearly reached me when I recovered my mind. I couldn't let them get past me.

---

[37] There is no historic evidence that Shamgar used this tactic. But if he did, it would be the right one when faced with an armed and armored enemy.

When I turned to look at the enemy I saw the lines milling and stumbling. Lowering the goad, I charged ahead of our men, and ran the goad into the back of a soldier.

While I tugged it free, our men were upon the enemy, frenzied. They clubbed and cut and slashed, while the foreigners were spinning and bumping into each other so badly that they were as ineffective as women. The town levies of commoners were entangled in the tethered horses and chariots, so that our men were among them before they could escape.

For myself, I have no clear memory of what I did. I know that I was jabbing and pulling and that, afterwards, my arms and back were sore. They tell me that I cut through the ranks of the enemy from the front to the rear, thrust through three charioteers, and cut back to the front again before working from side to side[38]. When we were finished, three or four chariots were seen going back to the city with mostly commoners aboard. The rest of the fugitives were on foot, scattered groups and ones and twos. I prayed that my smith might be among those who got away.

We let them go. We were spent. None of us had killed men before, and we were uneasy now that the frenzy was out of us.

We went among the dead enemy. A few were alive. We did as we would with a wounded animal, and gave them a quick death. When we counted the bodies, there were over six hundred dead Philistines in addition to some of the native people. We did not touch the bodies more than necessary, but we took their weapons for ourselves, and we left the bodies for the scavengers. We unhobbled the horses and let them go. There is no use for horses and chariots in the hills. We left standing

---

[38] In his wild battle fury, Shamgar could possibly have personally killed a great many Philistines.

the big shield with the image of Dagon. None of us would touch it. Then we went back into the hills.

And my life has changed. It isn't just that the foreigners don't come after our taxes for the time being. Our own people treat me differently. They say that I killed six hundred enemy soldiers with an ox goad. Did I kill that many myself? It is true that we killed more than six hundred. Those people who have kings say that their kings killed so many enemy, even though it was the armies of the kings that did it. We have no king. We have the LORD.

Still, some of the feeling of the Presence that came to me that day yet remains. The elders of our tribe come to me for discussion and even for decisions, and call me a judge. I farm my land and I listen to quarrels and troubles. My new ox goad is used only on the tough leather of my old ox, but everyone knows that if more trouble with the foreigners arises, we will fight and I will probably have to lead the way. But I hope I never have to kill men again, and I am afraid of that awful power that I felt on the day that we killed six hundred Philistines.

DEBORAH
Judges 4:7 - 5:31
One of the few women who figure prominently in the
Bible narrative. Deborah is
more of a prophet than a judge.

I just don't know how some men can be so dense. Oh, Barak came willingly enough when I called him, but he couldn't see what he could do even when I explained it to him.

Let's go back. I've been given the word of the LORD for many years now. It's not my doing. I only speak what I am told, but I can't tell you exactly how I'm told it. It began small enough, but the news got around that I could consult the LORD before I spoke, and elders from all the northern tribes -- Naphteli, Zebulon, Manasseh, and even part of Asher -- came with their questions and disputes. My husband Lappidoth was supportive, even though he doesn't have the sight. This meant that I could give the LORD 's word without charge and without bias. I think that I'm known as an impartial judge. Yet it's not me, it's the LORD'S doing.

In those days, Jabin king of Hazor[39] grew great. His city is massive and well fortified, and while our people had subdued the city when we took the Land, it was of no use to us and we let some of the people of the land return in peace there. In time, it became strong enough to be a kingdom. We should have destroyed it and sown it with salt, but that was before my time.

Another thing that was our fault was that our people took to the ways of Canaan, and worshipped their gods on the high places. I am grateful that our little hilltop was held by those who kept to the ways of the LORD, and no

---

[39] Hazor had been destroyed in the conquest of Canaan under Joshua, but apparently the Israelites did not occupy the city. By the time of this story, it had resurrected under Canaanite occupation.

idol ever profaned it. Our land had a large, solitary palm tree that bore good dates, due to the water seep in the dip below our hill. It was pleasant there, under the palm, and the tree and its shade could be seen from some distance. So that was where I went whenever the elders came to inquire of the LORD through me.

Our people took to the ways of Canaan[40]. This brought a curse upon us, as we had been warned. The curse took the form of Jabin and his general Sisera. For twenty years they lorded over us, taking tribute and demanding that we give them honor. I warned our people repeatedly, and some of them listened, but many did not. There was even an Asherah[41] pole on a hilltop that could be seen from our tent. And it wasn't just the men that were dense. Many of the women joined their heathen neighbors in the Asherah celebrations, shaming our nation. Yes, and I think that it was more of the women than of the men, mostly because of the fertility rites.

After twenty years of oppression, and after so many of the men who came to consult the LORD complained so much about Jabin and Sisera, the Word of the LORD came to me plainly. I obeyed. I sent for Barak, son of Abinoam of Kadesh. He did not have far to come, less than half a day's journey.

I told him, "The LORD, the God of Israel, says to you, ' Go, and take ten thousand men of Napthali and Zebulon,

---

[40] The various gods of Canaan were adopted by many Israelites. Collectively they were called "the Ba'al"s or (in the Hebrew plural, Ba'alim). The word literally only means "lord," and it was pronounced in two syllables with a glottal stop (that click you feel in your throat when you say "your aunt") between the "a"s. The main fertility god was often meant by the term Baal.

[41] The facts are obscure, but the Asherah appears to be the female consort or perhaps equivalent of Baal, and her cult symbol was a pole or a standing stone.

and lead them to Mount Tabor. I the LORD will lure Sisera and his troops to the River Kishon and deliver him into your hands.'"

Barak said to me, "That doesn't sound like Sisera being lured, it sounds like a suicide mission for me." I told him again that it was a command from the LORD.

Barak then said, "I know that you speak for the LORD, and I must obey. But since you think it's such a good idea, I want you to come with me. Perhaps the LORD will have another word for me along the way. I will not go without you."

"Very well," I replied, "I will go with you. But the LORD has told me that your attitude means that while you will conquer, you will not get the credit. A woman will take Sisera."

We went. I stayed beside Barak in the battle until the Hazorites broke up and fled. The River Kishon was in flood, and many men of Hazor drowned and many more were hampered enough for our men to catch them. Then Barak ran after Sisera and left me. I suppose that he was concerned about a woman getting to Sisera before he did. I had seen enough. I went back to my palm tree.

Sisera died before sundown. His army scattered northward toward Hazor, and Barak's men pursued and cut down most of them. Now, some years later, Hazor still stands but it is no longer a kingdom to fear. The Hazorites come no more to oppress us.

Barak broke off the pursuit and came to me before the night was over. He was never a proud man, and never a man to boast or assert himself. But he had the soul of a poet. He and I composed a song about how the LORD had destroyed Hazor, Barak was generous enough to give proper credit for the taking of Sisera. It was his idea to begin a stanza with,

> "Most blessed of women be Jael,
> The wife of Heber the Kenite,
> Most blessed of tent-dwelling women."

Barak now judges the land. He is the one who must decide hard cases on their merits, and he consults the LORD through me when the merits are not plain. He is also the one who must keep the men of military age equipped for war. We have had peace.

I sit under my palm tree and listen for the Word of the LORD. He still speaks to me, and I still give His word without price, and will until I die.

JAEL

Judges 4:17 - 22
The actions of Jael are those of both a reprobate and a heroine. Her husband Heber embodies the contradictions she dealt with.

My husband Heber has forgiven me. At first he was determined to put me away because I had killed one with whom he had allied, but he soon saw the way the wind blew, and he put on a public face of approval for my act. Still, it was a year or more before he would speak to me in the home, and more time than that before he was fully reconciled. Now he sees that I was right.

But he continues to apologize in the gate, when he goes to the city and the subject comes up, for my act of inhospitality. I had violated one of the most sacred obligations of a Kenite or any other tent dweller, killing a man who had sought our tent for protection[42]. I myself feel some guilt, although on the whole I would do it again. Sisera was a dreadful man. A Sikel he was born, and a Sikel he died[43].

I was against the move from the Negev to this green plain, even though it was better for our sons. I'm more at home in the desert. Heber thought that the king of Hazor was a rising star and that casting our lot with him was a wiser move than staying with the other Kenites. Indeed, at first it appeared that he was right. Soon after we moved, Heber became favored by Jabin, King of Hazor. Heber is not a small man among the Kenites,

---

[42] Throughout the Middle East among nomadic peoples, anciently and into modern times, the guest is sacred and is to be protected once he has entered the tent, no matter who he is or what he has done.

[43] "A Sikel." The Sikels were one of the Sea Peoples, and the name of Sisera is anciently known in the putative homeland of the Sikels, Sicily. In this story I've given him a helmet that the Egyptians recorded as worn by one of the Sea Peoples, a helmet with stubby horns.

and he has much property. He was invited to visit the great city, and he took his whole family to see the city of his powerful ally. Such a city it is! Great walls and gates, and more people than can be imagined in one place, all astir and going about business.

When war threatened, Jabin sent his general Sisera to see to the loyalty of the people who lived, as we did, just to his south. I disliked Sisera right away, but Heber thought that it would be good politics to cultivate him, so I held my peace. Sisera was no bigger than most men, but he affected the beard style of other Sea Peoples and he swaggered in gilded armor. He always wore a gilded helmet with ridiculous stubby horns, even in the tent. Heber didn't seem to notice that Sisera treated him with poorly concealed contempt.

At any rate, war came. Because we were Kenites, related to the Hebrews, we knew much of what was going on among the people of Israel. That put us not only between the contestants physically, but our loyalty was divided also. Jabin may have worried about us, but Sisera certainly didn't, and Sisera was the one who counted outside the walls of Hazor.

So Heber knew when the Israelite army was assembled at Mount Tabor, led by Barak of Kedesh and, of all things, by a woman. All this took place in such close quarters to us that Heber didn't go himself, but he sent a servant with a sealed message to Sisera in Hazor, telling him where the army was gathered and how many there were.   Then Heber thought it wise to take a small journey to Tyre, supposedly to buy a bit of scarlet cloth, but actually going only as far as the sea below Carmel. Heber is my husband and LORD, and I am committed to him, but sometimes I think ill of what he does.

Then the battle was engaged. We could hear some of the din at a distance, but the fighting didn't come all the way to our homestead.

Then Sisera, alone and clearly at the end of his strength, staggered to our tent. I suppose that he came to us because he knew Heber and considered him to be a friend. His gilded helmet was gone, and he had only his short sword. He wanted refuge.

What could I do? Heber was not home, and though I had most of the servants with me, I should not have invited a man into our tent. On the other hand, Sisera was nearly dead of exhaustion, and he begged admission. Would I hide him, he asked. I asked him where his army was, but he only motioned with his hand to show that it was scattered, so I said, "Come, my lord, don't be afraid," and let him in. I dismissed the few servants who were in the tent.

As soon as I dropped the door curtain, Sisera said, "I'm dying of thirst. Give me some water." Even then, he was as arrogant as ever. He stank. Not just man-smell, but the smell of terror-sweat, and I think that he had soiled himself. I had no water in the tent, but I gave him a draught from the skin of sour milk that was set aside to make cheese. I poured the rest out later.

Then he was concerned that someone might come in and see him, so I had him lie down and I covered him with a mat. He asked me to stand in the doorway and tell anyone who came that I hadn't seen anyone. He went to sleep.

Sisera was no more attractive asleep than awake. Soon his snores made it immaterial that he was concealed under a cover, anyone would have known that he was there.

I waited a little while to make sure that he slept soundly. Then I picked up a sharp tent pin and held it above his temple, and hit it with the peg hammer as hard as I could. Sisera jerked and began to quiver, but he made no sound. I hit the peg again and again, until I had driven it clear through his head and into the ground. His quivering stopped. Then I hit his head again with the hammer, feeling good to hit the revolting man who had compromised my husband and who had ordered me around like a servant.

It wasn't long before the men of Israel who were pursuing Sisera came along, led by Barak himself. I went out to meet him, and said, "You're looking for Sisera, aren't you? Come into my tent, and I'll show you the man."

Sisera lay where I had left him. I pulled off the cover, careful to avoid getting Sisera's blood on it. The carpet was pierced by the tent peg and bloodied, but that couldn't be helped. Barak and his men took away the body, and I waited for Heber to come home.

As I said, at first Heber was angry with me. This was tempered by the fact that all the territory was now controlled by Barak, who lived not far away, and it would not be good for Heber to show any loyalty to Sisera or Jabin. In the manner of pliable men, when Heber had to act as though I had done right his mind came around to agreeing with his actions[44].

Well, life goes on. Our sons prosper, and I'm glad to say that they are of firmer stuff than their father. The land here is good and our sheep do well. They keep me busy with their wool.

---

[44] This is the well-known phenomenon called by psychologists "the resolution of cognitive dissonance." Because his actions were forced in a given direction, his mind had to follow or he would be uncomfortable.

BARAK

Judges 4:6 - 5:31
Barak has a bad press for requiring Deborah to go with him. I choose to give him a better and a plausible reason for his taking her along with him.

I know what I can do, and I know what I can't do. I can put together an army, and I can keep enough of it together and fit over a span of years to maintain a defense for Israel.

I'm neither a judge nor a prophet. I no longer have Deborah to lean on, so I have to sometimes act like a judge, but no one -- certainly not I -- mistakes me for a prophet. What I do is done well. Of the things I was not designed for, I do what I must. I do not try at all what I cannot do at all. So I recruit and maintain and command an army, and now I govern like a judge. But I do not claim to speak for the LORD.

The LORD spoke to Deborah. He does not speak to me, at least not in a way that lets me claim to be a prophet. I go by what I know of the Law and about people.

And once -- just once -- the spirit of a poet came upon me. Together with Deborah, I composed and declaimed a great song. It was a great day, and I have never attained that height again. It was not in my character; it was the LORD. Our song is still remembered and chanted, but I don't have the voice for it any more, now that I am old. Then, in the flower of my strength, I chanted with the best. All things change.

Some folks scoff at me for taking a woman along on my first military campaign. "If you do not go with me, I will not go," I told her. It was not that I needed her as some sort of talisman, as the Ark was sometimes used to lead our fathers to victory, but I saw her as a necessary part of our command structure. She knew strategy. Or rather, the LORD gave strategy to her, and I carried it out.

So there was no point in leaving her sitting under a palm tree while I mustered an army and led it to the place she had pointed out. Why should we go in blind, when she could see?[45] And to be honest, I wasn't even disappointed when another woman got the credit for the victory. I knew, and all Israel knew, that Sisera's forces had already been defeated when he fled to the tent of Jael the Kenite. Credit is cheap.

Deborah told me where to take the army, and the LORD led Sisera's forces to the place of their slaughter.

The Kishon was in flood. Sisera's main might was in his chariot forces, and I could hardly believe it when they were delivered into our hands. Ought he not to have known that his chariots would mire down in the Kishon? Yes, but the LORD had blinded him. So on he came. When Deborah gave the word for our advance down the slopes below Tabor, I could see how our forces ought to be deployed. I deliberately thinned the ranks directly opposite Sisera's main advance, stacking triple reinforcements on our left flank. I told the center ranks to give way when Sisera approached the river, and to goad him into an all-out charge. Like the egotistic fool that he was, Sisera ordered a full attack. While most of his chariot forces were getting mired, I led my reinforced right flank into his vulnerable side, at a run. Our left flank came at his right flank, away from the shield arms of his men and at the side where an archer cannot easily shoot. Men on foot, like we were, are more mobile than chariots. When he tried to wheel to meet us, the horses became entangled in each other, and we poured in among them with our makeshift shields and with spears. As I had commanded, our troops ignored the horses except to hamstring a few in passing, and made the charioteers the first targets. So then the chariots, already disorganized, became unmanageable. The archers in the chariots were ineffective at such close

_____

45 Barak has a bad press, unjustified in my opinion. His reasons for wanting Deborah to go with him are, as expressed here, sound.

quarters, and the river did the rest[46]. The Hazorite troops, with their encumbering large shields and heavy armor, were of little account in the mud and water. We cut them down to a man. Our troops, fed up with years of oppression by Hazor, gave no quarter.

Sisera abandoned his chariot and fled on foot. We were delayed in mopping up his army, but we pursued him as soon as we could. I got to Jael's tent in time to pick up the body of Sisera. We had already picked up his abandoned shield and longsword. We never did find his helmet.

Out of breath, I sent my men back with the body and paused to rest. But I did not rest long. I went to Deborah, and started to praise Jael in a poetic chant. She and I then alternated in composing stanzas[47]. As I said, the spirit of a poet came upon me that day. It left me so drained that I am not sorry that it has not happened again. The song lives in our people.

King Jabin was shut up Hazor, his army destroyed. He had only his palace guard to protect him. Not "only," of course, because the high walls of Hazor were far beyond our power to take by direct assault. Jabin was safe, but he had the safety of a caged bird.

Deborah went back to her palm tree. I disbanded most of the army, but I replaced some of it with new recruits from farther away to the south. All Israel had lived in the shadow of Jabin of Hazor, and now that we had scored a victory over him, men from as far away as Judah came

---

[46] The Bible does not tell us Barak's tactics. However, any good general would have acted in this way, given the relative mobility of chariots in mud and lightly armored men on foot. I assume that the Kishon River did not suddenly send down a flood. It would be enough that the ground was boggy and Sisera was rash.

[47] The Bible only says that Barak and Deborah composed the song. But it would be natural to alternate the stanzas, and I elsewhere credit Barak with the praise of Jael.

to turn the tables on the Hazorites. Now it was we who roamed the country north of the Kishon, raiding Hazor's settlements as far as the coast of the Great Sea and even east of Jacob's Ford[48]. We were as merciless to them as Jabin and Sisera had been to us, and the booty more than paid for our soldiers' upkeep. So I was able to maintain a small standing army for some years. Hazor became of no account. We cut off its support base of villages and farms. There was no need to tie up our men in an actual siege. I have often wondered how Jabin spent his last years. Did he regret his persecution of our people? or did he simply see himself as a victim? I will bet that he never gave credit to the LORD. We did.

Deborah was older than me. I used to visit her regularly, almost every new moon unless my military duties prevented me. She continued to give me strategy, and of course she also continued her judgeship. Then she died. I have not been as confident since then.

My hands have been full. There is the army to maintain. More than that, it has been necessary to organize the tribal elders into some sort of unifying structure in Israel. I do that in a way that looks to them like a support system for our army, but the greater reason I do it is to give unity to the people.

The loss of Deborah was serious. She was the mainstay of our people's adherence to the Law of the LORD, while I used my system of elders to hold Israel together and to strengthen the people's devotion to the Law. It has not worked well since her death.

I can see the creeping loss of the Law. Reports come in of Asherah celebrations and of prayers to, or even images of, the Baals. I have had to confiscate personal idols[49] that were brought to the camp by a few recruits to

---

[48] Jacob's Ford is across the Jordan River just before it enters the north end of the Sea of Galilee. It still bears that name.

[49] I don't know that recruits carried personal idols. But judging from

my army, and now a standard part of our induction process is instruction in the Law.

It's a losing battle. When I join my fathers there will be no one to hold things together. This is not a military problem, because we have military peace. Rather, it is a problem of our whole way of life, made worse by the peace because there is no active enmity to show the contrast between our observation of the Law and the lawlessness of the local pagans. Would that our fathers had exterminated all the Canaanites and, when they came in, the Sea Peoples! Now they are a snare to us.

I am tired, and I miss Deborah.

---

the number of small statues and amulets that are found, some probably did.

GIDEON
Judges 6:1 - 8:52

Gideon is one of the best-known judges. The Bible seems to give him three different personalities: a simply obedient man, a self-determined man, and an apostate. I've tried to weave these contradictory characteristics together.

Many mighty things have happened to me. I have seen the Angel of the LORD face to face and I challenged Him in my bitterness, and He let me live.

But when my children ask me, "What is the greatest thing you remember?" a different scene rises before my eyes. I am standing in the enemy camp, miraculously undetected, and listening to two Midianite men. Though I normally understand only some words in their language, it is as though they were speaking in the Hebrew dialect of my tribe. "I have had a dream," one said, "A loaf of barley bread rolled into the camp, struck the tent, and the tent fell." "That can only mean the sword of Gideon, the son of Joash. The LORD God of Israel has delivered us into his hand," his friend said. At that moment my life changed. Until then I had moved at the LORD'S bidding like a man in a dream. Suddenly I was awake and saw what I was doing, and the strength of ten filled me. My life was set on its path that I could see. Other people think that it was always clear. I know differently.

We all lived in fear of the Midianites, who swept through the land like locusts. They went where they pleased, and they took what they pleased. We of Israel were simply their prey. They camped everywhere. We were powerless to fend them off, and we hid what we could and scraped by on meager rations. We tried to help each other; if it were not for that, none of us would have survived. We had no king, we had no guide, we had no hope.

The Midianites are nomads and they roamed at will in those days. They had no real home, only a desert to the east and south where they went between raids. In the Land, they lived as nomads live anywhere, and everywhere was home to them. They treated the Land as their own, and considered our crops to be only their right. This they did in those recent days. Now that the LORD has struck them with the sword of the LORD and of Gideon, they keep to their desert, those who survive. They lived by the sword, and their fate was just.

You who lived in enclosed cities have no idea of how it was for us in the open country[50]. We hid in caves when we had to abandon our homes, we planted small plots of grain in places that were hard to get to, and we hid our pitiful harvest in pits.

Some of us knew why we were so helpless. A man of God wandered through the Land, warning us that we were destroying ourselves with the worship of Canaanite gods, especially the Baal of the harvest. Some of us listened. Others redoubled their devotion to Baal. My father, a leader in our clan, had an image of Baal and an Asherah pole. The harvests were poor, and the Midianites took most of what we did reap.

I knew the source of our trouble. The man of God was right. You have heard that I first took action against Baal worship in my own town. Did I do that as my own idea? Of course not. I was one of those who hid from Midian, threshing my grain in a winepress to hide it, when the LORD spoke to me. "The LORD is with you, mighty warrior," He said. How would I know that it was the

---

[50] Most of Israel was rural at that time. Town people usually had walls or at least a large enough number of men to discourage raiders. Country people would be vulnerable. Israel at that time was not an organized entity, but a collection of nearly nomadic herdsmen and very small farmers. The country was studded with remaining Canaanite villages that were more powerful than the farm villages. Raiders, especially mounted on camels, would be able to roam with no organized opposition.

Angel of the LORD? No, I thought it was only some dignified stranger. So I challenged him in my bitterness, because I was indeed bitter. I said to him, "If the LORD is with us, why are we in this trouble? Where is this LORD now that we need Him? We hear wonderful stories about what the LORD used to do, but now He has abandoned us." And He let me live. I called Him "my Lord," because my father had taught me to be polite to strangers, not realizing Who He was[51].

He turned to me and spoke in His Name, and I still did not know. Oh, by then I knew that He was no ordinary stranger, and I prepared an offering. Not quite sure of Who He was, I prepared it so it could be either a meal or a sacrifice. He told me to put the offering on the rock, with no wood, and touched the rock into flame with His staff. Then He vanished from my sight, and I knew. And He let me live.

His Voice stayed with me. "Destroy your father's image of Baal," the Voice said. I felt strange, hearing a voice as though it were both in me and in front of me. "Make a sacrifice to the LORD on a proper altar with your father's bullock." Was I to defy my father? But the Voice could not be disobeyed.

With ten of my men, I went at night and did as I was commanded. Then I went home before daybreak and told my men to be silent. Of course, someone talked, and the other men of the place came to my father and demanded my death for blasphemy. Blasphemy against a wooden image! My father had heard the prophet who was warning Israel against Baal worship, and although it was his images that I had destroyed, he told the men of the place, "If Baal is a god, let him contend for himself."

---

[51] The text is pretty ambiguous about Gideon's understanding of who had visited him. It reads like a gradual increase of understanding, from regarding the visitor as just a passer-by to recognition of Him as the LORD or a messenger of the LORD.

And that is how I got the name of Jerub-Baal[52]. And the men of the place saw reason, and they also let me live.

The Voice would not leave me alone. I was filled with -- what? -- a spirit, the Spirit of the LORD. This was a new thing. Me, the man who hid from the Midianites, was commanded to go and conquer them.

Like a toy before the command of the Voice, I blew the trumpet and had it sounded through my own clan of the Abiezerites, and then had it blown throughout the tribes of Manasseh and Asher. It was a measure of our people's desperation that men gathered to me with what weapons they could find. The tribes of Zebulon and Naphtali also responded[53]. We were a host, if not an army. There were thirty-two thousand of us. This action took the scattered Midianites by surprise, so that they were not able to prevent our assembly. They could only assemble themselves and prepare to destroy us.

Then my fear returned. Could I lead this host, who covered the Land as far as I could see, and who had brought only enough provisions for a few days? How was I to organize them? I temporized. I told the elders of each clan to take charge of their men in the way they would at home, and I went off to seclusion at the winepress.

The Voice followed me, or rather it hovered over and in me. Yes, it is true that I asked for a sign, and then for another sign. The fleece that people talk about really was wet, and then dry. I told the clan leaders about it

---

[52] The name means "strive, Baal" or "let Baal strive." In other words, let that pagan idol defend itself.

[53] Why did Gideon take men from only a few tribes? Probably because communication in those days was so poor that it would take forever to muster the whole nation. And there was need for haste. The "army" had to be assembled before the Midianites could counter-muster and destroy them.

afterward, to strengthen them, and they were strengthened. Remembering the prophet, and the destruction of Baal, and now this miraculous sign, the men formed up behind me and we marched north. Well, we didn't properly march, we walked as a crowd, not in ranks. We didn't know how to form ranks, and ranks wouldn't have worked in this rough country. We were faster as a host.

The alarm had gone through the Midianites who were scattered over the Land. They had gathered in the valley near the hill of Moreh. They were far more swift than we, mounted as they were on camels and accustomed to breaking and setting up camp. So they made a formidable group. Our scouts (I did have enough sense to send out scouts) told us that they numbered over a hundred thousand.

Then the Voice broke into my plans before they were even clear in my own mind. "You are too many," it said. Too many! Here we were, an untrained host of men, outnumbered by three or four to one by the trained Midianite raiders, and the voice told me that we were too many! I was still moving in the grip of a force that I didn't understand, and so I obeyed the Voice and told the leaders that any man who was afraid of the Midianites should go home. Most were glad to have the excuse for getting out of a hopeless fight, and my "army" was cut down to a third of its beginning size.

I looked at my now ten thousand men, one tenth or less of the number of Midianites, and the Voice spoke again. "You are still too many," It said. So I took the men down to the brook to drink, and as the Voice commanded, I selected the mere three hundred who lapped from their hands. I didn't know then, and I don't know now, why that was the sign. Still moving at the word of the Voice, I sent all but those three hundred home, keeping the supplies of the ten thousand. I was glad later to have those supplies, because we needed those grain jars, and as you know we had to pursue the enemy for days in the strength of what we had.

It was not I who decided to visit the Midianite camp. Moved by the Voice, I took my trusting servant down there. And the great thing happened. I heard the conversation of the Midianites, and I awoke. The Voice no longer needed to impel me. I went back to our encampment and called, "Get up! The LORD has delivered Midian into your hands! Empty three hundred of those jars[54] of parched grain, and put a lamp in each. Quickly eat and drink, because we have to begin the fight before dawn." So I divided my men into three companies.

Remember, I was awake now and the thoughts came to me without the Voice. In me still was the conviction that the LORD was with me. I felt as though my head would burst with the greatness of what we were about to attempt. I set men over each of the three companies and sent two of the groups beyond the Midianite camp. I stayed on the hill, where my light could be seen. Long before first light, at the beginning of the third watch, I broke my jar, poured oil on the lamp flame in a handful of straw, and blew my trumpet. Instantly, fires flared up around the Midianite camp and the sound of trumpets and cry of "For the LORD and Gideon!" filled the air.

You have heard of the chaos that the LORD sent upon Midian. They thought that we were a full host and that we were all about within their camp. They started up from sleep and cut down anyone whom they encountered in the dark, hacking blindly at each other. Those who could do so ran out of the camp, and we had to let them go. We went into the camp and thrust through any Midianite who still lived and secured the

---

[54] Where would Gideon have found 300 jars so quickly? The obvious answer is that he had had the dismissed troops leave their rations, which would have been jars of parched grain or bulgar wheat.

camels that had not been ridden off. The Midianites were now without provisions in a strange land, and they were straggling toward the Jordan to escape.

Men from Napthali, Asher, and Manasseh were still armed, having been sent home only a day earlier. They pursued the Midianite stragglers, waiting for them at the fords of the Jordan. I sent word south to Ephraim, asking them to hold the southern fords of the Jordan while we all hunted down the Midianite survivors. Ephraim complained about not having been invited to the first battle, but how could I have gathered a force from so far away without letting the Midianites preempt us? So Ephraim accepted my apology. They had loot enough. Even the camels of the Midianites were adorned with gold.

Meanwhile, I and my three hundred men, and others who joined us, pursued the Midianites who had been the swiftest because they had taken time to mount their camels during the panic below the hill of Moreh. If the LORD had not strengthened us, we could not have kept up the pursuit. The cities of Succoth and Peniel refused to give us food and water, and you have heard how we repaid them on our return.

So we took the two kings of Midian after the last battle at Karkor, and brought them back and executed them.

The men of the tribes said to me, "Rule over us, you, your son, and your grandson." Now, it has never been done so in Israel, that a man should be king and that his son should be king after him. So at first I refused. I was content with the portion of the loot of Midian, a gold earring from each man who had taken two.

So now I am rich. The Voice does not speak to me anymore. Apparently I am no longer needed for a great enterprise. I wish that the Voice would return, but it is empty to ask for what cannot be had. I must do as I see fit. I am no longer filled with that bursting sense of mission and power that I felt at Moreh, either. We shall see.

I had to find something to do with all that gold. It was as much as a man could carry, and I could not spend it all on ordinary things. With most of the gold, I made an ephod[55], and set it up here in Ophrah. Sometimes I wish I had not done that, but I cannot now change matters, because men from all Israel come to worship, and I need it to hold the tribes together. The work of rulership is not difficult, but the tribes are quarrelsome. As to the LORD, I try to shape the minds of the people to recognize Him and to abandon the worship of the Baals. I am still Jerub-Baal. The priests at the Sanctuary have my full support, though their influence is dependent upon those who make the prescribed festival journeys to the Sanctuary. Some of the Levites are faithful to the LORD, some are not, and many of the people are indifferent now that we have peace. During that brief time when we struck down Midian, there was zeal for the LORD.

I am still rich. I did not need more land, now that we can work our whole farms without fear of Midian, and gold is not as scarce as it was while it was worn only by Midianite nomads and their camels. I did buy a house in Shechem, and bought a concubine to keep it. She has a son, Abimelech. My other sons do not want him or his mother, but I am the father, and my son is my son.

Meanwhile, the men of Israel would not be denied. They insisted that I rule over them. I can at least give them that for now. It appears that it will work out. I have many more sons. If they turn out like my son Jether[56],

---

[55] We don't really know what an ephod was. Maybe it's just a general term to denote any sacred object. But the tone of the Bible seems to be disapproving where an ephod us mentioned other than the one associated with the High Priest's breastplate. Gideon seems to have done wrong here.

[56] Jether did not succeed Gideon; see the next story. Abimelech did

we need not worry. He is gentle but wise. I would like him to succeed me, but he lacks ambition. Well, I lack ambition too, but in my time I had the Spirit and the Voice.

---

succeed him, and he was neither wise nor gentle.

ABIMELECH
Judges 9:1 - 57
Abimelech can certainly not be considered a judge, if by that we mean a man who represented the judgment of God to the people. He is admirable only if you like strong and aggressive egocentric men.

I am well named. My father Gideon, better known as Jerub-Baal, named me for his own purposes. He meant my name Abi-Melech[57] to mean "My Father is King," meaning to memorialize the kingship of his LORD. I choose to see the king as being Gideon himself, and for me to have the boast of being his son. I have a hereditary right to the kingship.

Also, I have a base, this city Shechem. It can be rebuilt. It is an ideal base for a kingship, and here in my city I actually am king. It is well fortified, it has good water. And it had the famous sanctuary of Baal-Berith[58].

This sanctuary was a key to my kingship. I am not a religious man, and one Baal is the same to me as any other. But this Baal-of-the-Covenant is politically crucial, because it is in his sanctuary that the covenant of the cities and towns in this area was kept and renewed. Without it, I would have been hard pressed to hold the confederacy together.

I have needed all the center-holding power I could get in these divided times. Men have always held against me the politically necessary act of eliminating the competition. Yes, they were my brothers, but only half-brothers, and certainly not citizens of Shechem. So,

---

[57] We are accustomed to pronouncing it "Abim-elech," but the true division is between "Abi" (Father) and "Melech (King)," so it should be "Abi-melech. No problem - - it isn't the only Biblical name that gives us this trouble. In English, the pronunciations we ordinarily use will serve OK. Not many of us speak ancient Hebrew.

[58] "Baal-Berith" means "Baal (or lord) of the Covenant."

after the unpleasantness at Ophrah[59], my city mostly overlooked the manner of my taking power. My one regret is that my half-brother Jotham escaped and made that inflammatory speech from the mountain. People forget bloodshed, but a clever orator can leave an annoying camel-thorn under the robe.

The first three years of my rule went well enough. Then worthless men of Shechem set up robbers' nests in the surrounding hills, interfering with trade against my express commands. It was necessary to lead troops out of the city to suppress them. Then that troublemaker Gaal came, and he and his men stirred up Shechem against me. But my loyal city governor got word to me, and I took all my army out to the heights around the city, with headquarters under the soothsayer's tree. When Gaal was forced to make good his boast against me, and sallied out of the city to meet me, I destroyed him and burned the city for good measure. The burning of the stronghold in the city deprived me of a future refuge of my own, but it had to be done. I am a practical man.

There was another unfortunate unintended consequence. The sanctuary of Baal-Berith was also burned, together with its covenant documents. But they were only parchment; those sub-kings who had made the covenants with me will remember. If not, and if I cannot make them remember, I will have no kingdom anyway.

So now I am taking my army off to Thebez, where the sub-king has renounced his covenant with me. The city walls themselves will not be too much of a problem, partly because I have made it a policy to know the details of each of my subservient cities' weak spots. The inner tower will be difficult to take, but we can starve

---

[59] This "unpleasantness" was Abimelech's slaughter of all but one of his half-brothers. This was a brutal but common way of assuring that there would be no rivals to the throne of the city.

them out if we have to. I want to keep that tower[60], because I intend to make Thebez my new capitol.

---

[60] As we learn later in the Bible's story of Abimelech, it was from this tower that a woman dropped a quern (house millstone) onto him in the siege, and this was the cause of his death. He asked his men to finish him off so that it would not be said that a woman killed him. So much for kingly ambition and pride.

TOLA

Judges 10:1,2

We are told virtually nothing about Tola except his name, his tribe, his residence, and how long he judged. So this one is made up of the whole cloth. I have chosen to make his dual tribe membership the center of his role.

Abimelech was dead. While he ruled Israel, many of our tribes went their own ways, leaving to the house of Jerub-Baal[61] and of Abimelech the bitterness and murder that centered on the north, in Shechem. There were many of us, here and there, who dealt with the judgeships of various tribes. I became the leader in Ephraim.

I am of the tribe of Issachar, and I had moved south to Ephraim at the beginning of the troubles in the house of Abimelech. Being from another tribe, I was trusted to be impartial among the clans of Ephraim, and thus I could be an elder who had no biases. This, I believe, is one of the main reasons I became recognized as a leader.

When Abimelech died, the leaders of the tribes came together to select one man to be chief judge among all. We knew that, if we did not unite in some way, outside forces would overwhelm us again, as had the Midianites before the day of Jerub-Baal.

We were, we who had arisen to prominence in each our tribe, mostly faithful to the LORD. The common people, on the other hand, were faithful in some places and in other places they worshipped the gods who are no gods, the gods of the people of Canaan and of lands beyond. This is the way it has been since our fathers came into the Land, except when oppression and trouble forced them to seek the LORD. We who carry responsibility

---

[61] Jerub-Baal was the name given to Gideon (see Footnote 43). Later he was called Jerub-Bosheth, with the abominable name of Baal replaced with the word for "shame." This may have been true by Tola's time.

have to know what has taken place, and we have to think about these things. The result is that we realize that the LORD, He is God. And that Midianites and other plagues come when we depart from His ways.

The leaders chose me to be the judge of Israel. I was, again, partly because I, as a man of two tribes, was less likely to be a biased judge. Because we tribal leaders are many and because I am the one chosen, I do not have to judge the Land alone. I am chief, but I do not forget that the others and the LORD chose me. Only when a tribal judge cannot resolve a problem because it involves another tribe do I have to intervene. When I do, I act through my fellow judges in their own tribal areas. It is better this way, better for them and better for me.

It has not been a burden. I conduct my own affairs, and do the judging while I am in the city gate in any case. So far, nothing unusual has been brought before me. It is all routine, thanks in part to the other elders who advise me.

JAIR

Judges 10:3 - 5

Jair and his sons seem, on the basis of the Bible text, to have been primarily the rulers of the cities of Gilead, northeast of the Jordan. Jair's "judgeship" is marginal in his career.

Gilead is a good country. We are occupied by parts of the tribes of Gad and Manasseh, but we are not as tribal in our organization as are the people west of the Jordan. I and my thirty sons are the real powers here, controlling thirty towns all the way from the Jordan to the desert to our east. And our influence extends westward well beyond the Jordan

The Jabbok River gives us water and a travel route from the high desert to the valley of the Jordan. Another trade route passes through our Gilead, north and south behind the crest of the steep hills that overlook the Jordan. We do well for ourselves.

In spite of their tribal loyalties, the Israelites west of the Jordan depend upon us for at least some semblance of unity. By "us" I naturally mean me and my sons. We have spread out, from our base here in Gilead, to exert influence all the way to the foothills that overlook the Great Sea. We have not actually built homes there, but we have established trading depots, fanning out from the Jordan opposite the Jabbok. The result is that, when Tola died, it fell to us to carry the responsibility for communication and commerce, This led, naturally enough, to responsibility for arbitration and for decisions that involve the whole Land. It is helpful that the Sanctuary is not far from the mouth of the Jabbok valley.

As I now near the end of twenty years' rule, I can see signs that things will not go well in the Land. The Sea Peoples are stronger, and they have been settled in fortified towns such as Beth Shean near the Jordan valley. They are flies in the ointment. They have the support of Egypt, that walking corpse that still has enough soldiers to overwhelm us if they wished. They do not wish. The Land is a good land, but the parts that are best are too far off the main routes to be worth the trouble for them. So they settle mercenary colonies of the Sea Peoples, mostly the Philistines, where they can do the most good for Egypt. Egypt thinks that they own the Land. We generally ignore them.

So, with minimum effort and with not a great deal of impact, I and my sons give Israel all the rulership that it needs and will accept.

I do not involve myself in religion. The religions of the people are too diverse and too contentious to deal with directly. I support the Sanctuary, and I leave the worshippers of the other gods alone. There is profit in peace.

JEPHTHAH
Judges 10:6 - 12:7
What are we to think of this man, Jephthah? Otherwise ruthless, he feels bound to a foolish vow. His inner conflict and his misery for the next six years must have been awful.

I never thought that I was of much account. No one ever tried to tell me differently, either. To everyone, I was "the Bastard," the son of a prostitute[62] in the house of a father who had legitimate sons. It was considered somewhat of a marvel that my father took me in and raised me. My brothers were not so generous.

Some of my brothers were older, and some were younger. When my father was not present, it was "Bastard this," and "Bastard that," and "Bastard, you are no brother of ours." They had kind words for me only when there was something that they couldn't easily do. I was strong and I worked hard. Though my father and sisters treated me well, I became bitter and untrustful.

It came to a head when my father was old and simple. My brothers banded together and took me to the elders at the gate. "This bastard is the son of a prostitute, and we are sons of our father's wife. Allow us to expel him!" The elders called for the local Levite and consulted the Law. "We cannot forbid you to do that, but we warn you that you are not treating your brother properly," they finally said. So I was sent away. I was not given any of my father's inheritance, being allowed only a change of clothing and supplies for a journey.

Since my people didn't want me, I went to Tob, which was allied with the Ammonites. It was a lawless place, and a life of persecution had made me strong and quick. I soon made a name for myself, and no one cared

---

[62] Jephthah was raised in Shechim, apart from his brothers who lived in his father's main household. This seems to have colored his whole life.

whether I was legitimately born or not. I became a chieftain in that turbulent land, finally commanding a substantial troop of men who, like me, had little to lose. Admittedly, we made part of our living by raiding the sparsely settled lands to the east, but we also established ourselves as farmers and traders. I married a girl of Tob.

Then our daughter was born. Her mother died bearing her, but she lived long enough to say, "Her name is Beulah[63]." And Married she was to be. I bought a wet nurse and raised my daughter alone. I never fancied any other woman after my wife died.

Some time later, when my daughter was nearly old enough for marriage, word came from my former home at Gilead. The message was from my brothers, no less, carried by some of the same elders who had agreed to my banishment. At first, knowing who had sent the messengers, I refused to see them. But they were urgent.

I had an idea of what they wanted. Ammon was making war on Israel, and there was something the elders wanted the bastard to do. I and my band of men were now known widely as formidable fighters, and the elders of Gilead wanted us to fight the Ammonites for them. The Ammonites were too strong for the tribes of our people.

The first message was that I could now claim my share of my father's inheritance. So he had died. I was sorry to hear it, but I had not seen him for over fourteen years. I told the elders, "Let my brothers keep the inheritance. I don't want it. I have made my own inheritance here."

---

[63] The Bible does not tell us the name of Jephthah's daughter. I've chosen to call her Beulah, which means "Married" in Hebrew. This name symbolizes Jephthah's hope for her and makes her premature death all the more poignant.

They shuffled a bit, and then came out with it. "We want you to be our leader and fight the Ammonites," they said. I had thought so.

"I have no quarrel with Ammon," I said. "If you come and lead us, we will make you our head, and you will rule us," they offered. I'm not a trusting sort. "You don't mean it. If I go back with you and fight Ammon, and the LORD gives them to me, will you really make me your head? If you do, I will hold you to it as long as I live." "No, but we will make you our head," they pleaded. So I made them swear on their beards, on their fathers' names, and on the Sanctuary. And I went back with them to Gilead.

While I was getting the men of Gilead into fighting shape, using my own men as cadre, I tried diplomacy. I sent to the king of Ammon, asking what he had against us and why he was fighting us. He replied that we had long ago taken his land, and he wanted it back. I sent another message, pointing out that we had taken it from Sihon, king of Amor, not from Ammon, that it was the LORD who had given it to us, and that it was too late after two hundred years to want us to give up the land. "Will you not keep any territory that your god Chemosh gives you? and will we not keep the land that the LORD has given us? Have other kingdoms, such as Moab, tried to retake the land they gave up to the LORD?" I didn't expect an answer, and I didn't get one.

Then the spirit of the LORD came upon me -- came upon me, the bastard! -- and I gathered the fighting men and Gilead and Manasseh to attack the Ammonites. I was finally a man of honor, and I didn't fail to acknowledge that the battle was in the hand of the LORD. I sent a message before me to the king of Ammon, saying, "Let the LORD judge between us."

Moreover, I made a vow[64]. We were going into battle, we were near enough to see the host of the Ammonites with their Moabite auxiliaries, and I am both a proud and a hasty man. I felt that I should say something to inspire the men, and I proclaimed, " LORD -- if you give the Ammonites into my hands, whatever first comes out of the door of my house to meet me when I return in triumph from the Ammonites will be the LORD's, and I will sacrifice it as a burnt offering." I knew that the LORD was with us, but I wanted to say something. The LORD heard me, and the leaders of the army heard me. How often in the past three months have I relived that proclamation! It echoes in my ears.

There is little more to say. We fought, and the LORD gave us victory that day. We cut down the Ammonite army and pursued them, destroying twenty towns that sheltered them. In less than a month we had subdued Ammon.

I led my men back, and we passed my home. I had not given much thought to the vow I had made in the heat of war, and then disaster fell on me. It was my daughter, Beulah, who came out to meet me, leading her maidservants and dancing to the tambourine. The last thing I had thought of, and it should have been the first. I had thought that it would be something or someone who was a significant sacrifice, maybe my old ram who was always patrolling the southern boundary of my land. Or my steward, driving a kid of the goats before him for the welcome feast. But my daughter!

In front of my men, who had seen me so strong in battle, I fell to the ground and tore my tunic. I poured dust on my head and wept. I could not speak, and only groaned,

---

[64] Why would Jephthah make such a foolish vow? First, consider that he was a rash and impulsive man. Then, he is in the grip of excitement of the coming battle, and all his men were looking to him. At such a moment some stirring speech was in order. So out comes this rash vow.

"My vow! My vow!" I drew my sword to fall on it, but my men restrained me.

It fell to my chief lieutenant to tell my daughter about the vow. She, a gentle creature and the only child of my loins, had come first to meet me, and now she was dedicated to the LORD for sacrifice. I could not look at her.

My daughter came and tried to raise me up. I would not. She said, "Father, you have given your word to the LORD. Do to me as you vowed. Am I not a small thing compared to the deliverance of Israel from Ammon? The LORD has avenged you of your enemies, the Ammonites, and you return to your home with honor. You must keep your vow."

Then I let her raise me up, and I wept on her shoulder. I, who was a warrior, wept. And she said, "Give me this, please. Let me take my friends and roam the hill with them for two months, mourning that I will never be married and give you grandchildren. Then I will return."

My men were waiting for me. I said, "Go." And I let her go.

I, however, had to lead my men on to Gilead and fight Ephraim[65]. Two months were spent in more fighting. The men of Ephraim accused me of slighting them by not asking for their help against the Ammonites. I said to them, "I did call on you, but you didn't come in time for the battle. Why do you want to fight me?" I was tired of fighting. Ephraim paid no more attention to my offer of peace than had the king of Ammon.

---

[65] His quarrel with Ephraim fits well the two months that his daughter asked for. Jephthah, with an army dependent upon him, cannot take a vacation to tend to family matters if he wants to hold the army together. So he has to take care of Ephraim. He will have six years to live with his grief and guilt.

We fought. Ephraim was no match for our trained and seasoned warriors. We held the fords of the Jordan and cut down everyone who tried to cross over and who betrayed the speech of an Ephraimite. Forty-two thousand men died. And for no purpose.

I had no rest. Even facing the tragedy at home, I was persuaded to lead Gilead. They had made me their head, and I would not turn back.

So it is time. My daughter Beulah whose name says that she was to be married has returned satisfied in her mourning. Tomorrow I must offer her to the LORD. She is at peace. I am not, and I never will be.

I cannot ask a priest to do what I must do. I have to do what I have vowed. "Do not bind my eyes," she told me. "Let me look on you. I am not afraid." And she is not. I am.

I have resolved what to do. I have seen enough death to know how. When I raise the knife, it will be first a quick thrust to the heart before I make the cut of the sacrifice.

Then she will be gone. For the sin of my vow, I will remain. The years stretch ahead of me, barren and heavy. I am the last of my line. There is no other child, nor will there be. The burden of the people's need for me cannot be laid down. Would that my men had not prevented my release on that dreadful day when I came home! My daughter, my daughter! Would that I could die for you!

IBZAN

Judges 12:8 - 10
Ibzan is another judge about whom we are told little. In making him also from the whole cloth, I have made him a stickler for the Law, literal and fundamental.

I didn't exactly inherit my judgeship, but it didn't hurt to be the eldest son of the most prosperous Levite in Bethlehem of Zebulon[66]. My father was advanced in years when he died, so I myself was beginning to show gray in my beard when I inherited his home. I had only one brother, who of course got one third of the inheritance. He settled down to being a small herdsman, taking his turn at the Sanctuary and being, shall I say, of not much stature.

I had already made somewhat of a reputation as a student of the Law, and I was skilled as a scribe. I had made my own copy of the Book of Moses[67]. It had taken me the better part of five years between my other duties, but it was a magnificent set of scrolls if I do say so myself. It was the only complete one in Bethlehem.

Consequently, even in my middle age the elders had come to me for readings from the Law when difficult decisions had to be made. Because I had studied the Law and had written every word, meditating on each precept, I became recognized as one of the elders while my father was still living. My estate enabled me to spend most of my time in the gate. I was well known for the precision of my judgments.

---

[66] Not Bethlehem of Judah, the Bethlehem with which we are most familiar. This was another town of the same name.

[67] This writing out of the whole Law would be in keeping with the character of a rigid and punctilious man such as I have imagined Ibzan to be.

With Bethlehem being one of the chief cities of Zebulon, all the difficult law cases in the territory came here for settlement. We elders -- may I say, "I?" -- would deliberate, consult the Law, and deliver our opinion. Shortly after my father's death I was recognized as the chief elder of Zebulon. It wasn't long before other tribes brought their inter-tribal disputes to us, and I questioned them and stated the decision. Then the tribes brought problems that they had been unable to resolve, even if they didn't involve more than one tribe. So I became the recognized judge of Israel.

It was not really burdensome. The Law itself is clear, and I had only to apply it. Most of the time, everyone was satisfied with my judgment. If a man had to be physically punished, I made sure that the strokes stopped at thirty-nine. The result was that only a few were disabled for any length of time, and the people acquired a healthy fear of the Law as I declared it.

Oh, there were a few times when I had to make unpopular decisions. I remember one young man, who was less than seventeen years old, who had been heard to mumble a curse at his mother when she had scolded him. The parents themselves had not reported it as they were required by the Law, but two neighbors had heard it. I had to disregard the acknowledged fact that one of the neighbors had previously been hostile to the family, and the other neighbor had testified reluctantly. It was clear that a curse had been uttered. Both parents interceded for the young man, and the mother wept bitterly when I delivered my judgment, because there was no previous report of disobedience by the young man. But the Law, as I said, was clear. The young man had to be stoned to death. When the time came for execution, many of the men of his town had business elsewhere, and the rest threw the stones too lightly. I had to step forward and show them how, so that they would not be at it all day, even though at my age I could not strike a fatal blow with a large stone. Then they put their arms into it, and the Law was satisfied. There was much grumbling against me for a while.

My care for the Law worked in the other direction also. A man was brought to me by a group of his neighbors, elders who turned out to be zealous to follow the instructions of Moses but not fully informed. They told me that this man was a heretic and deserved punishment, perhaps even the death penalty. Their charges were cumulative, and they added up to the accusation that this man violated the legal customs of Israel. I sifted the accusations one by one, and it was plain that the man was unpopular for good reason. He was stubbornly independent and he antagonized all with whom he had to do. I felt justified in lecturing the man on his behavior. But none of the charges in itself was enough for legal action to be taken.

Finally, the one clear accusation was that this man had a heterodox house[68]. Instead of having the normal three long rooms and a broad room (the design that facilitates ritual cleanliness), his house consisted of a central room divided half-way, with doors that led to the rear two rooms. To get to the other rooms, one had to go through two successive rooms. Thus they claimed that this man was necessarily a Law-breaker regarding separation of the clean and unclean. It became plain that the elders were misinterpreting a building custom as though it were in the Law. I showed them that Moses had made no such requirement, and that I believed the standard house layout to be only a custom, though a sound one.

---

[68] There is much that is argued about the Israelite occupation of Canaan. But one thing on which there is agreement is that a particular house design, the four-room house, shows up at this time in the archaeological record wherever the Israelites are expected to have been. The house plan was of a larger room in front and three smaller rooms against the back wall. It is speculated that this plan facilitated ritual cleanness by keeping one of the rear rooms reserved for clean and one for unclean purposes, with no need to pass through the unclean in order to reach the clean.

The Law did not allow me to exact punishment. So I sent the elders away with a stern admonition to quit making laws that were not the Law, threatening them with penalties for religious arrogance. I told the man himself that he would be wiser to either move to another location or remodel his house. I told him that, if a charge of actual uncleanness was proved against him in the future, I would exact the penalty. The Law, once again, was sufficient.

You see, a judge has to be definite and unshakable. I take my time to arrive at a judgment, but once I make the decision, I am adamant. If a judge is uncertain or if he wavers, the people will not follow him.

I was as fair as the Law of the LORD allowed. Every time I had to make a judgment, I went to my scrolls and re-read the portion that applied. Then I read it aloud to the elders, and explained its application to the case. There were some who would cite other passages or otherwise try to contradict my interpretation, but I never yielded to them. My devotion was to the Law, not to men. The LORD had spoken.

All this time, I prospered under the LORD. With two wives and several concubines, my family was too large for just my father's house even before he died, and my wealth allowed me to establish several adjoining houses. I was strictly impartial to my wives and concubines, as they bore me thirty sons and thirty daughters. I got no joy from some of them, but they sufficed. I found wives for my sons, and gave my daughters in marriage, outside our clan[69]. By that means I established a wide-spread set of family relations that covered almost all of Israel, especially after I became judge of the whole people. These family relationships did me a great deal

---

[69] It is a long-established practice in the Middle East to cement political ties by marriage. This would facilitate any judge's ability to influence the whole nation without limitation by tribe.

of good and helped in my prosperity, so it was plain that the LORD had prospered me.

Altogether, I am well satisfied with my status as judge of Israel. Now that I am getting old, having been judge for nearly seven years, I will join my fathers in peace and contentment.

ELON

Judges 12:11, 12
Elon also is given only a few words in the Book of
Judges. It would be natural for the
successor of the legalist Ibzan to be different from him.

When I became judge of Israel, Ibzan of Bethlehem of Zebulon had just died after ruling Israel for seven years. As to the Law, Ibzan's example would be hard to follow because everyone considered him to be without peer in his ability to find and cite the rules behind his decisions. So I took over in the shadow of a great man.

On the other hand, Ibzan was known as a hard man, maybe too hard. His family ties reached all over Israel. In fact, I still rely on the family network he established, and I count many of his relatives as my friends and use them to communicate throughout Israel. I could never be as influential as he was in matters not related to the judgeship, but I do my best to be a fair judge. There had been a lot of grumbling about Ibzan's severity, and I myself had often thought that he went too far, so I strive for a middle ground.

Being a judge is not only difficult, it is a heavy burden. There is the responsibility of interpreting what the LORD has said and seeing to it that the proper application is made and that justice and equity prevail. There are times when I agonize over a decision, and I often have to discuss the case at length with the elders. Fortunately, our town is blessed by the LORD with steady and intelligent elders, who are a great support to me and without whom I would be much less at ease.

There has been a continual troubling of our Land by the descendants of the people who lived here before the LORD took it for our fathers. We beat them back, and I as judge am the one who sends out the call for men of war and who appoints the military leaders. I let the military leaders decide military strategy, and the LORD is always with us. I invoke His protection daily, as do the priests at the Sanctuary.

The most troublesome incursions are not by the native peoples, but from the coast of the Great Sea, in the form of the Sea Peoples. They have been establishing themselves along the coast. The worst of them is the Philistines, but they are south of here and I only know of their depredations in relation to the military actions I have to call out in Judah and its neighboring tribes. The Philistines are so prominent that, in the south of Israel, all of the Sea Peoples are simply referred to as "Philistines." Closer to us in Zebulon are the Sikels[70] and their allies. We have been able to contain them, thanks to the LORD.

But the really hard thing to deal with is the apostasy among the people of Israel themselves. I understand that it is no longer as bad as it was in the days of judges such as Gideon, but any amount of it at all is a threat to our existence as a distinct people. Much of my judging involves this apostasy.

It is hard to enforce the Law when so many people disregard it. The worst is that many of our people have mixed the old Canaanite worship with that of the LORD. They will set up a hilltop shrine, declare that it is for the worship of the LORD, then carry out worship ceremonies that look a lot like the ones their Canaanite neighbors hold. I can do little about this, partly because those who are faithful to the LORD are reluctant to turn in those who have strayed.

But sometimes things go so far that I have to step in. A while ago, it was reported that a hilltop shrine had not only standing stones[71] but also a cast statue of a bull[72].

---

[70] These are now known to have settled along the more northern coast.

[71] Standing stones were used to represent many different gods,

This was a day's journey south of here, and I felt that I had to go and see for myself.

When I arrived, several local men and elders had gathered to meet me. The man who had set up the shrine defended himself, claiming that he was only trying to focus his worship of the LORD by using a symbol of the LORD's majesty. I understood his intent, but it was clearly against the Law to make any graven image, whether cast or carved. I called the elders into a circle, and argued the case. I quoted from memory the Law that was carried from the Presence by Moses (blessed be his memory). The owner of the shrine also argued his point. Then we discussed it. The case was open and shut. Though I had the authority to declare the judgment myself, I arranged for the eldest of the local elders to speak the decision. The man had to have the bull melted down into negotiable metal pieces[73] and for good measure he had to take down the standing stone. Then he had to promise to go to the Sanctuary within the year and to make the prescribed sin offering. The local elders saw to his faithfulness.

It is a continual task to encourage the people to go to the Sanctuary at Shiloh for the set festivals. Many are conscientious, but many are not.

So I work my work, trusting in the LORD.

---

apparently. The old Canaanite chief god, El, seems to have been represented by a standing stone or pillar, and the Asherah (a poorly understood, probably female, deity) had a standing stone or a pole. The records on this next are meager, but it does appear that standing stones were mixed into the worship of the LORD.

[72] Just such a bull statuette has been found in a hill shrine.

[73] As noted earlier, there were no coins at this time, and metal was weighed out for valuation.

ABDON
Judges 12:13 - 15
The third judge is a series that is given a total of only seven verses.

Being a judge is a little like being a king, except that you don't have as much power as a king. You can advise, and cajole, and command. And the people will pay as much attention as your reputation requires. They will go ahead and do what they always do, unless they see that you're really speaking in the name of the LORD. They can see it, and if you tried to act as though you had the LORD 's word but you really don't, they'll just go on and ignore you.

Sometimes they ignore you anyway. Then there's nothing you can do but let them go, and pray that not too many innocent people suffer from their recklessness. A king would not put up with that. He would command, and enforce his judgment if necessary. A judge has no palace guard.

I became a judge in the usual way. Even while Elon judged from Zebulon, I knew that I had the mission of speaking the word of the LORD. My father Hillel was a prominent man here in Pirathon, and he was a nephew of Ibzan by marriage. After my father became too old to sit in the gate, I took his place as the chief elder of Pirathon, and I grew accustomed to settling disputes and validating the judgment of the other elders. Because I was connected with the network of families that had been set up by Ibzan, I was able to spread my influence into the other tribes, until I was recognized as the judge of Israel after Elon died.

Ibzan was too strict, too formal. Elon was maybe too much the other way. Yes, I know that the same LORD was behind both of them and me, but I've found also that the person is given the freedom as to how he is to state the LORD 's will. So I have tried to check the Law for my judgments, listen for the inner guidance of the LORD, and temper my statements of the LORD 's will to suit the circumstance. I do not bend, but I try to be gentle.

Once in a while, the LORD speaks to me in a dream. This is unusual, and it generally means that some matter will come up that I had not previously known about. Sure enough, a stranger or a delegation will arrive with a problem that relates to the dream. When this happens, I still wait a day before making a decision, and it has been my experience that almost always the judgment is agreed to by the appellant.

True to the legacy of my great uncle Ibzan, my family's prosperity has enabled me to run several households. In addition to three wives, one of whom died young, I have had six concubines. I am able to maintain a household for each of them. I have forty sons, several daughters, and now thirty grandsons. Believe me, providing enough donkeys for them to ride has been a financial drain! As soon as a son became twelve years old, I gave him a donkey, replacing it as it aged. The grandsons more or less expected the same of me, and I have been happy to give it.   Sometimes I think that I am single-handily supporting the donkey breeding business in this area[74].

I followed the example of Ibzan in marrying my sons and daughters out of the tribe, so now I have my own network of relatives to administer my judgeship throughout Israel. That considerably relieves the burden of my judgeship.

I mentioned the times that the LORD plainly and specially gives me the word to declare. At other times I consult the book of the Law, having followed the example of my great uncle Ibzan in this too, that I copied out my own

---

[74] The writer of the Book of Judges surely must have enjoyed the humor of a man having to provide donkeys to forty sons and thirty grandsons. Was that original writer Samuel? Probably.

scrolls. I also talk the case over with the other elders of the city, and particularly consult the elders of the town from which the case has been brought if they are present. In some cases, I have sent for the elders of the town if they have not come to me, and in a very few exceptional cases I have traveled to the place where a dispute or a need for judgment has arisen.

For seven years now I have been judge. My years sit heavily on me, and I feel that my time will not be long. Thanks to the LORD, my ears and my mind have not aged as much as the rest of my body and no one has requested that I step down from my judgeship.

SAMSON

Judges 13:1 - 16:31
What went through Samson's mind in those last moments, as he prepared to bring down the temple of Dagon on the heads of the Philistines and on his own? Samson's was a long career, and I've chosen to have him think back on only the highlights.

If I can just get to those pillars. They think that I'm only a big, dumb animal, but I'll show *them*[75].

I've learned, in this past year. I've learned to control myself and to not let them know what's been happening to me. It's been the hardest thing in my life -- and, until this year nothing was hard for me. This year has been hard, so hard that I wanted to die and I thought that I really would die from how they treated me. Forced to grind at the mill like a donkey all day -- it was worst at the beginning, before my strength came back. Eating my poor food by feel, in a bowl on the floor, like a dog. Sleeping on stone, on a scattering of foul straw. I hate them.

Now they're finished with me for today. They poked me with spear points to make me jump, they hit me with sticks, and they made me try to catch them. I had to pretend. That was the hard part. I, who could easily tear up the stone floor and smash them now, I had to pretend that I couldn't catch them. I even heard them send in a little kid with a sharp stick to poke at my legs, and they laughed when I groped above his head. I knew.

---

[75] We don't usually think of the Philistines as great thinkers. However, their material culture was far advanced over that of the contemporary Israelites. We have no surviving records of how well or abstractly they thought, and for that matter we don't know their original language, though we may have good reason to think that it was similar to ancient Greek. But in view of the cultural difference, Israelites may have felt a bit of inferiority to the Philistines except that they were pagans. So I've let Samson boast, perhaps out of a gnawing doubt.

I know where I am. They've put me in that round area in front of the pillars, that area with its low stone rim like a hearth, more than two arm spans across. And they made sport of me like an animal.

A blind animal. My eyes! my two eyes! But in my mind I can still form images. The pillars are red.

I saw them more than a year ago. I was in this same temple. I asked questions, and I see things. I can't see now, but then I *could* see. It was quiet then, not filled with these whooping people. Well, they're quiet again now, and I can hear the priest chanting in front of that image. I can see him in my head. He wears that silly fish cape[76], with the tail dragging behind him and the head sticking straight up.

Back then, when I was accepted in this city, the priest was happy to show me the temple from the doorway, where we could see how it was put together[77]. I see – I *saw* -- and I can think. I know something about buildings. How many times have my neighbors asked me to lift roof beams into place. I know how things fit together. Above the pillars, the main roof beam is divided, and the rest of the roof is carried on that great two-part beam. All the other beams rest on it. We have no buildings like this at home, but the idea of roof beams is the same. Only we don't have that big opening above the central area. I can feel the sun on me now.

---

[76] There is an ancient Mesopotamian carving of a priest of Dagon wearing such a cape.

[77] In spite of the fact that archaeologists have found the ruins of only one possible Philistine temple, which shows hints of this pattern, I've chosen to describe it as a variant of the contemporary Mycenaean palace. This would explain how Samson was able to pull down a building by pushing only two columns. In the Mycenaean Greek palace, the round area would be a hearth, with the smoke hole above it.

The priest told me then that the temple is put together something like the king's house. I saw that too, when they first brought me bound from home. There, the round area really is a hearth, which explains that opening in the roof above it, and there are four pillars around it. The king's chair is against the back wall, where that ugly statue of Dagon stands in this temple. But four pillars or two, that's what holds up the roof and the second story of the building.

I see other things in my head, just as plain as if I had my two eyes. Delilah. I see that woman as she was when I first met her, beautiful and sensuous. I haven't had a woman for a year, not since they took me to Gaza. I hate her. She came to see me once, after I was blinded, and she tried to tell me that she had been forced to turn me in. She cried. That woman can cry. Once, her crying and whining was what moved me to break my vow. No more. I hate her.

My vow. I never made the vow. It was my parents that made it, and I went along. Yes, I know that it was the LORD who told them to do it, and I certainly know that what the LORD says must be obeyed. I did obey. It was a bargain. I got to be a hero, and I wore my hair long, and I was allowed to do great deeds, before I broke the vow and my strength left me.

I hate these people. Once I just brushed them off. I could beat them with my hands tied behind me, and I did. I killed dozens of them. Now I hate them. No one knows the terrible pain of being blinded. They took me to this very spot, in this round area in front of the pillars, and the same priest chanted as he pushed the point of his knife into each eye. The world flashed into two great bursts of light and into unbearable pain, then it went dark and it's dark now. I can still see the last thing I saw -- the point of a knife, while my eyelids were held open. I hate them[78].

Then the prison. Around and around the mill, pushing that pole with me serving as the donkey. At first, the task felt heavy, but they hit my back with a rod if I slowed down. I hate them. I'd grip the pole in my two hands, and hate them. I quit cursing them after a while, because they just laughed and struck me harder. I couldn't reach them.

Then I got stronger. I can think. So I pretended that the work was as hard as before, and I plodded around the mill. I grew stronger as my hair grew -- what does hair have to do with strength? though with me, it does -- and one day a little while ago I gripped the pole and felt the wood yield under my fingers. Then I knew I had to pretend a little longer.

I never used to pretend. All my life, I did and I said just what came to mind. I could do anything. I was smart, but no one noticed that because I was so strong. You think it's easy figuring out how to catch foxes so you can tie firebrands to them? Or how to charm your way into enemy cities and families when you want something? Or when you just want to do it because you can? I'm smart.

Everyone respected me, but it was only because I was so strong. They never thought that I could use my mind. All right, so some of them feared me more than they respected me. When I was little, other kids teased me because of my long hair. That stopped after I gripped one of them by the wrist and felt bones snap.

I did whatever came to my mind. When that lion challenged me, I tore him like a rag without giving it a

---

[78] Before, Samson was only contemptuous of the Philistines. The pain and humiliation of being blinded must have inflamed him and provided the focus of his life from then on.

thought. But it took thinking to make a riddle out of it, and I made a good riddle. I'm smart.

I was careless, because I could be careless. Nothing stopped me. I even got to the point where I bossed my parents around, though I never disrespected them. "Get her for me," I said. And they did. It was the first woman I had for myself, but there were more. I can't figure out women. They all seem to want me because I'm so strong. *Was* so strong, and I'm strong again. Every time, I trusted them, and every time they betrayed me. Well, it's too late now to use what I know about women.

I hate these people. My hands itch for the feel of bodies and blood, as I felt when I killed them in my strength. Lawless, arrogant, violent, oppressors of my people when it suits them. But who am I to talk? I've had my share of arrogance and violence, and then I became a lawbreaker about my vow and my hair.

Did I not know in my bones that she would betray me if I told her about my vow and my hair? I knew, but I was arrogant. I actually thought that I could still be strong and invincible forever. Tears, woman's tears, but it was my vow that broke.

The priest's chanting is rising in pitch. It's time.

Boy, take me to the house pillars so that I may lean on them. I'm a poor old prisoner and I feel weak.

Here they are. The fluted plaster over the cedar posts is smooth. And it's red, I remember that it's red. I can easily place a palm on each pillar, they're so close together.

The priest's chanting has stopped. My mind sees him turning around to face us. My fingers dig into the plaster on the pillars.

Just once more, and then let it be over! Great LORD, give me this, just once more! Then let me die with the Philistines.

Now! Now! Avenge me, LORD! For my eyes, my two eyes![79]

---

[79] And the building came down, with the mass of people who were on the roof. Samson killed more Philistines in his death than he did during his life, the Book of Judges says.

The Mother
Judges 17
This indulgent mother has no better understanding of theology than does her son Micah, and probably the same misunderstanding as her neighbors.

My husband knew that he would die soon. There was blood when he coughed, and he was too weak to go to the fields. So he told me what to do with his estate.

"The farm will support you and Micah," he said. "My steward is an honest man, and he works hard. See to it that he gets his due. The silver that you and I know about -- it is all that I have gathered in a lifetime of toil[80]. Keep it hid against the day that our son Micah has a male child, so that we will know that my line will continue. Then give it to him. If he has it before then, he is too likely to waste it. He has so little sense of responsibility. A dreamer! and we need a farmer. I am leaving instructions that you are to manage the household, and not Micah. Not yet. Wait until he has a male child."

He died. I did as I was commanded by him. It is hard enough, but I am frugal and our steward is indeed a man to depend on. Would that Micah were like him!

And the day came, when Micah was full grown and married, but yet with only a girl child, that I went to check the silver, and it was gone. All of it, all the fruit of a lifetime of toil and careful management, gone.

I am a quiet and simple woman, but when I saw that we had been robbed, I surprised even myself with my outburst. I ran screaming into the courtyard, and Micah and the steward and Micah's wife ran in to see what was wrong.

---

[80] This man must have had a large farm with servants in order to have accumulated as much silver as this story reports.

I called down a curse, calling on the LORD to witness. "May the thief pay seven-fold in suffering! May he get no good from his theft, may all his crops rot! May he live to see raiders ravish his wife and kill his children before he is maimed and blinded! Let the curse of a poor widow cling to him and infest him with boils that cannot be healed! LORD, give me justice and destroy the man who has taken away the inheritance of my son! As the LORD lives, may He fall upon this man with disaster!"

The steward and Micah's wife tried to comfort me. Micah turned pale[81] and began to tremble. Even in my grief, I could see him shrink as though a knife were twisted in him. We spent the day, each in our own distress.

At evening, after we had tried to eat a meal of boiled grain with a bit of lamb, Micah came to me. He carried a sack and begged me to call back the curse. "As to the money, I took it. Here it is, I give it back to you. Only call back the curse. I am afraid of a curse in the name of the LORD."

"But why did you take it? I just kept it hidden so as not to distress you. Was it not yours? Did you not know that only the fact that you do not yet have a male heir has kept it from you?" I wanted to know what had led him to take the silver without telling me.

"But I didn't know it was so much until I found it and felt its weight[82]," he said. "Then hunger for the silver came upon me, and I took it from its hiding place. And when I

---

[81] In modern times we don't put much faith in the power of a curse. But in those days, and in many places even now, a curse could literally kill the person who was cursed and who believed in the power.

[82] The amount of silver is given in weight, eleven hundred shekels. The modern equivalent is about 28 pounds, a very considerable amount for those days.

had taken it out, I could not bear to put it back again, and I couldn't tell you because of my shame. Now please call back the curse."

I did. I even gave him back the sack of silver, even though it was against my husband's orders. I wanted to ease his pain and fear. Besides, I was tired of the responsibility for the silver. Perhaps his wife's second child would be a son. She had already shown her fertility with a daughter. And so I gave Micah the silver, and I told the others in the household that it was all right, the silver had been set aside for Micah anyway. I said to him solemnly, "The LORD bless you." So the curse was called back.

I still felt uneasy about the power that I had unleashed in my grief and anger, and I told Micah that he should dedicate the silver to the LORD by making images. We had a silversmith make two images, so that we could worship the LORD in our own home instead of having to journey all the way to Shiloh. They are handsome images, too, both overlaid with silver[83]. Now we have a household shrine.

We are simple folk here in the hill country of Ephraim. So it was an event when a young Levite came through. I do not know all of what he and Micah discussed, but the

---

[83] We don't know what these images were like. They were probably of wood overlaid with silver, because Micah used only about five ounces of the silver for them. The story is clear that they were supposed to be aids to the worship of the LORD and not Canaanite gods. The Bible and archaeology agree that the Israelites of that time did make images that were intended to represent God. In most cases the images were of bulls, and in both Samaria and Dan in later days images of bulls were used to represent God as aids to the people's worship. Clearly, neither Micah nor his Levite saw them as forbidden graven images that would violate the Law. Evidently they interpreted the commandment to forbid the making of images that represented a god who was not the LORD. This event was early in the Israelite occupation of the Land, and theology was not yet fully clarified.

end of the matter is that now the Levite lives with us and conducts our worship with the aid of the images.

It is just as well that Micah has the silver. I wish he were as industrious as our steward, but one cannot have everything. Micah is good to me, and I wonder if he still carries some fear of my curse. Well, I worry about him. He is not as strong a man as was his father.

Our steward does most of the running of the farm. His family is also helpful, especially now that his sons are old enough to work in the fields. It is a comfort to talk with his wife. She is younger than I, but she is an understanding woman.

Micah spends too much time in the gate. Or he will sit long after time to go the fields and discuss matters with our Levite. I don't begrudge him that. It is good to have a son who in interested in religion.

As for myself, I am getting along in years now, being well over forty. I will leave this life soon[84]. Until then, I rejoice that Micah has a good wife, and that we no longer have to go to Shiloh -- not that we went there often, but now we don't have to go there at all.

---

[84] Most women did not live long in those days. For that matter, men also were old at fifty, but women seem to have had a harder life than men and they mostly died much earlier than now. Let us assume that she died before the Danites took the Levite and the images.

A Willing Young Levite
Judges 17:7 - 18:31
Clearly, not all Levites were scholars of the Law.
This one was an opportunist, and no scholar.

Bethlehem of Judah was good enough, I suppose, if you have no great ambition. Being a Levite there means having a secure life, except for raiders, but there are so many sons of Levi[85] there that I was like a single locust in a swarm. So I went afield to seek my fortune. I was young then, and I owed nobody anything, since my older brothers had the bulk of the inheritance[86].

The first few villages on my way north were not much different from Bethlehem. Oh, Jebus[87] was a big city, but in that Canaanite fortress there is no place for a Levite, so I merely passed it by. It was only a quarter days' journey from home, anyway.

As my way led north, the novelty of my status became evident. There are Levites in certain places in the Land, but I was off the beaten path much of the time, where the farmers seldom saw a Levite except when they went to the Sanctuary at Shiloh -- if they went there at all. So I lived well on their hospitality. My limited learning was not evident to them, though it was to me, and I had not brought any scrolls of the Law.

---

[85] The "sons of Levi" were the tribe of Levites. The Levites of Israel were members of the tribe that had no area of inheritance in the Land, and were positioned in various specific towns. Their inheritance, the Law said, was the LORD. They were supported in their religious work by the other tribal people, and by their own work.

[86] It was not uncommon for younger sons to leave the family area and seek their fortune elsewhere. The eldest son was entitled to half of the estate, and other sons had to divide the rest. During the life of the father all sons shared in the family life, but some would have thought ahead like this young Levite.

[87] We know the city of the Jebusites as Jerusalem, Jebus Salem. It owns its existence in this dry land to the presence of a perennial spring, the Gihon, in the Kidron valley below the old hill town.

So it went for some months. With no fixed destination, I could afford to move at impulse. I worked my way up into the hill country of Ephraim.

It was there that I encountered Micah, a man of some substance. When he asked me where I was from and where I was going, I answered him that I was looking for a place where I would be welcome and where I could settle down. And that I am a Levite.

Micah invited me in and treated me as his guest. There turned out to be two very good images[88] in his house, and when I asked him about them, he told me that they were to aid him in worshipping the LORD of Israel. "They aren't necessary," I told him, "the LORD does not need images and He is death on the images of the Canaanites." "But these help me to worship, and besides they are totally different from the gods of the Canaanites. They aren't gods, they're just representations for the LORD."

I was going to lecture Micah about images, when he said, "You're a Levite. Stay with me and be my priest. I'll give you ten shekels of silver a year, with the first year paid right now, and your food and clothing[89]. You will be part of my household."

I could use the silver, and this looked like what I had been seeking. Micah was not leaving the worship of the LORD, after all, and the images were just images, not Canaanite gods. Perhaps I could turn this into some good, even though I had only my memory of the scrolls of the Law and had not had much formal training. So, after a few days of discussion, we struck a bargain. I

---

[88] See footnote 55 above.

[89] These were fair wages for that day, when life was simple and set of clothing lasted for a year.

would serve as priest, and Micah would acknowledge that the images were not themselves gods. They didn't resemble the images of Baal or the ridiculous Dagon that I had seen in other shrines. All would be well.

We prospered, Micah and I. We made an ephod[90] to go with the images. We rejoiced over the birth of his first son, which he took to be some kind of a sign. In due time, his mother died and was buried. Micah's growing family took up the space. We were on good terms with the neighbors, many of whom came to take part in worship. I considered two or three of the local girls, but didn't choose any of them just yet.

Then came the Danites. They were only five of them, and they came to the house to spend the night. When they heard my voice in worship, they must have recognized what I was about, and they told me that they also recognized my accent as not one of Ephraim. So they took note that I was a Levite, and found out that I lived with Micah and was his priest. They said, "Please inquire for us of the LORD as to whether our journey will succeed." I asked them about it and cast the lots. Then I told them, "Go in peace. Your journey will succeed." So they left, and I thought that we had seen the end of it. Time passed.

Then the Danites really came, this time as a host of six hundred men[91] and a baggage train   Their tents covered the hillsides and the valley. We all were uneasy, knowing from various reports that Dan had not settled down into their promised inheritance in the Land. What if they wanted the hills of Ephraim?

---

[90] See footnote 55 above about ephods.

[91] Six hundred may not seem to us to be much of an army. But not all tribes were large in those days; this story seems to be quite early in the occupation of the Land by Israel. See the story of the re-founding of the tribe of Benjamin by the remaining six hundred men (Judges 20:47 and 21:14-23).

But only one man, the leader, came to the door with the five men who had been to Micah's house before. They said nothing, but the five men went in and picked up the silver images and the ephod and went out.

All six hundred armed men then massed behind them. I said, "What are you doing? Do you think that you have the right ..." And the leader said to me, "Be quiet. Don't say anything. Just come with us -- do we not have the images now? -- and be our priest as you have been here. Isn't it better to be the priest of a whole clan and tribe than to be priest of a little household?"

They not only had the power on their side, but what he said made good sense to me. Wasn't it indeed better to have a whole tribe to serve? Would I not prosper even more? And what did I leave behind? I had no roots with Micah. So I said nothing, and stepped forward and picked up the images and walked through the line of shields and into the army.

Micah came out of his house and blew the ram's horn trumpet of alarm. We of Dan struck tents and moved off, with the families in front and the army in the rear. We had only gone a short distance when Micah and the neighbors he had summoned caught up to us. Micah was shouting and waving an ax.

The leader of the Danites, called Abi-Dan, halted and waited for Micah to catch up. They spoke together. Then Micah went home. He could see where the power lay.

As for me, along the way I led worship of the LORD from time to time, whenever we paused long enough to spend the night. The Danites had not had any Levite cities, since they themselves had no territory, and I was the only Levite they had. Indeed, I was the priest and father to a whole tribe.

We came to Laish. I took no part in the battle, aside from blessing the army before the fight, and I stayed away from the scene until the mess[92] had been cleaned up. Bloodshed unnerves me, and I am a Levite who must keep some sort of purity. It would not do for me to touch a dead body.

We settled in, and renamed the place "Dan" in honor of the tribe. I was furnished with a house with a shrine large enough to hold the images[93] and the tribal leaders for worship. We established an altar in the open, so that all the people could witness the worship. When it was dedicated, I declared in a loud voice, "This is the dwelling of the LORD, the LORD who brought you up out of Egypt and into this fair land," and many other great words that came to me. If I say so myself, it was a good speech.

So I am truly enlarged. I am surrounded by an armed camp, in which I am the only Levite. They have given me my choice of wives, who has borne me two sons already. The Danites shall have a household of Levites, and the means for worshipping the LORD without the need to travel south to Shiloh.

---

[92] The Danites took the defenseless city of Laish and killed everyone in it.

[93] In much later years, I Kings 12:28-30 records that the first king of the Northern Kingdom of Israel had golden calves (bulls) made and he set up one in Dan to compete with the Temple in Jerusalem. The tradition of that kind of worship may have persisted at Dan.

Micah

Judges 17:1 - 18:26

Micah is an example of what went on frequently during the time of the judges and later, setting up images on "high places" and thinking that they could thereby worship God.

I never expected it to be so much[94]. My mother had always held down the household expenses and had constantly reminded me to work hard so that we would have enough, and here was a fortune. Oh, I had always known that my father had left me some silver, and that it would be mine when a son was born to me. But I expected it to be a handful or so.

This was a big sack of silver that I had found. Evidently my mother had hid it right in the house, under a slab of rock by the hearth, and I only found it when I noticed that the stone was tilted and needed to be laid straight.

There was no way to get it hidden again without leaving signs that the stone had been moved. The silver was mine, and I might as well take it right then, even though I did not yet have a son. But how could I tell my mother that I was taking it before the time? Better to let her think that it had been stolen.

I wasn't ready for what happened when she came in from the fields and saw that the stone had been moved.

Her screams brought all of us running. Then she called down a curse on the thief, not knowing that it was I who had taken the silver. The curse was heavy, and full of power. She was wild with the force of it, and she called on the LORD. It was a curse that would stick[95]. She

---

[94] See footnote 82 above. This much silver, some 28 pounds, would be a fortune for those days.

[95] Both mother and son believed that such a curse would work. Micah was in real danger.

didn't know that it was I whom she cursed, and that the consequences would fall on her own household. I knew. I was terribly afraid. On top of my guilt for causing my mother such grief was the certainty that her curse was powerful, and that it would indeed fall on me.

It was a long afternoon of distress, a distress that drove all of us away from each other. After we had tried to eat without success, I came to my mother with the sack. "It was I who took the money," I told her, "Now please, take back the curse. I am afraid." I was really upset and still trembling.

"May the LORD bless you, my son!" was what she said. And she took back the curse. May I never have such a weight as that curse on me again.

And so, and it was her idea, I had her take some of the silver to the craftsman, who made two images. Perhaps if we dedicated that much of the silver to the LORD, he would not let the curse fall on me. So the images were made and overlaid with silver, and installed in a shrine I had made in the house. Now, with a shrine for His worship here in our house, the LORD would prosper us.

The Levite came. It was good to see a man from another tribe, from far away at Bethlehem in Judah. There was much that we learned from him about how that tribe lived and how they farmed. The Levite also knew something of the Law of the LORD, and we talked about Him. At first, the Levite was uneasy about the images, but I explained that they represented the LORD to us, and that they helped us to worship.

And I got an idea. Here was what we needed to really have a fully functioning shrine. I persuaded the Levite to stay with us, and to be our priest. I made him part of our family, though he did prefer to spend some time alone. I did not even expect him to work on the farm. He did do some work in the fields, but that was at his wish. It was enough for me that he was our priest.

We prospered. We saved ourselves several days' working time each year by not going to the Sanctuary at Shiloh, where the Ark is. We had our own shrine. The men of the area came to the shrine also, and the Levite and I became influential men in the tribe. A son was born to me. Unfortunately, my mother had not lived to see him, because she had died not long after I had found the silver.

The Danite spies came. They conferred with the Levite, then went away. A few weeks later, the whole tribe of Dan came, going north to claim a homeland. They were fierce people, never having settled down in the Land after our fathers took it, and fully six hundred of them were equipped for war with armor, shields, and spears. It was a force to be afraid of. I carefully covered the hiding place of the remaining silver and we stayed in our inner rooms, calling the steward and all his men in from the fields. We put our flocks into the pen behind the house, and we waited.

The spies came right into the house. We knew them, and so we were not afraid of them, but the armed warriors stood outside the gate. The Levite went to talk with them. Suddenly they picked up the images and the ephod and went out with the Levite, and went behind the ranks of warriors. There was nothing I could do.

As soon as the Danites left, taking my Levite and my images, I blew the trumpet. Men who heard me repeated the call, and many neighbors rallied to me, bringing what weapons they could find. We set out after the Danites, and caught up with them beyond the first spring.

The Danites stopped, and their warriors formed ranks. My men stopped, too. I was angry, and I went forward as the leader of the Danites came to meet me.

"What is the matter with you, that you come out with your men to fight?" he asked, smiling as though he didn't know what I had come for.

"How can you ask what is the matter?" I yelled at him, "You take my images and my Levite! They are all I have! And you ask me what is the matter?"

The Danite leader still smiled. "Don't shout at me," he said quietly, "or some of my men may lose their tempers. Why should you and your family lose their lives? Go home in peace."

What could I do? We were maybe thirty farmers with sickles and axes and ox goads, and they were hundreds of armed men behind shields.

We went home, and the Danites and my Levite and my images went north.

I am destroyed. My gods and my Levite are gone. I have an empty, useless shrine. The LORD does not hear me. And I cannot get justice. We have no king[96].

---

[96] The last sentence of the Book of Judges is "In those days, there was no king. Every man did what was right in the sight of his eyes (or, as he pleased)".

Abi-Dan

Judges 18:2 - 31
This attempts to give a voice to the leader
of the tribe of Dan, a man who must have existed.

They call me Abi-Dan. That's not my real name, of course. The people gave it to me after I had become the chief man of the tribe of Dan -- the "Father of Dan[97]." I encourage the use of this name. It is a help to me in maintaining leadership in this hard and bitter tribe.

It was a hard struggle on the way up. We of Dan have never had it easy. Joshua gave us a section of the Land that was particularly hard to conquer.

On the east, we were squeezed into a narrow strip between Ephraim and Judah. We were assigned a broad strip of the coast of the Great Sea, but what good was that? There in its center was the fortress city of Ashdod[98], with its high walls and its large contingent of fierce Philistine warriors. We fought. We were always at war, from the day we first tried to take our territory. It did no good. Our resources were continually drained by the fight with the Philistines, and there was no hope of taking Ashdod. Whoever held that city would hold the lower hills, the fertile coastal plain, and the coast.

We had come into our part of the Land with reasonable equipment for war, but the Philistines had a limitless supply of men and weapons. The ships of the other Sea Peoples began to bring in quantities of iron weapons[99],

---

[97] "Aba" in Hebrew means "father." The Bible does not give a name to this man, so I have given him a cognomen, a name assigned to him by his peers.

[98] Ashdod was a powerful city in those times. Perhaps then, perhaps shortly after, it was one of the five chief cities of the Philistines. It is not likely that the tribe of Dan could take it.

[99] At about that time, the Sea Peoples flooded into the coastal area and brought the new technology of working iron. This gave them a

and then we knew that we had lost. We established small ports where we could, and tried to do sea trading, but we were squeezed out by the Sea Peoples[100]. Two generations in the Land, and we still lived like nomads, and now this new metal that could cut through a bronze sword. We had to move.

I called together the elders of Dan and we tried this plan and that. Nothing seemed workable if we stayed in this unwinable territory. Each of our tribes had been assigned its territory, and the other tribes were settled in. Yes, there were raiders among the other tribes, and the Philistines sometimes plagued them, but they each had a secure territory. We could not find a place in the Land; it was filled by Israel. We had to look farther away.

No hope of settlement south of the River of Egypt[101]. The troops of Egypt were too mighty for us, and they were on the alert because of the invasions by Sea Peoples. To the west was the Great Sea. To the east, beyond the settlement of the tribes of Gad and Reuben was the desert, not worth the taking. But there might be space to the north. We would see.

And so we chose five men to go north beyond the Land and scout it. They came back in due time and told us about a fertile valley with huge springs of water that made a river flowing into the Sea of Fresh Water. It was called Laish[102]. It was not a fortified city, but a wide

---

tremendous military superiority over those who had only bronze.

[100] The Sea Peoples were maritime powers. The Bible has an obscure reference to Dan and its ships. I have chosen to weave that into an unsuccessful attempt by Dan to play the maritime game.

[101] This is not the Nile, but a small river or wadi that marks the northern boundary of Old Egypt.

[102] Laish was renamed Dan by the tribe after they took the city. To complicate matters further, the Bible also calls the city Leshem (Josh 19:47).

farming community with many towns. One town, the one bearing the name of Laish, was fairly large but it had no real walls. The people of Laish were careless of their safety, and had not been alarmed when our tribes took the Land from the Canaanites. Perhaps they knew that Moses had not assigned their territory to any of us. They also felt secure, our scouts reported, because they depended upon the power of Sidon to protect them in case of trouble. What they seemed not to know, and what our trained scouts could see, was that the coastal mountain range between them and the Great Sea was enough of a military barrier that the Sidonians[103] could not reach them in time if there was an invasion.

And an invasion it was to be. I gave the word. We were already well organized. We had to be, what with all the fighting we had been doing. And we had never settled down in one place, so we simply broke camp and moved north. We would have a little over a week of travel, with all our dependents and all our baggage, before we reached Laish.

Less than two days into our travel we came to a place that our scouts knew, the home of a prosperous man in Ephraim. The scouts told me, "Do you know that this house has an ephod, household gods, and two silver images?" I said, "You know what to do." We had no treaty with any of the other tribes, and we were a strong fighting force.

I stayed behind the spies as they entered the house and went to the chamber of the shrine. It was near the entrance gate, a separate chamber that was also the house of a Levite. My armed men stood behind me, a spear's cast back. The Levite, dressed as a priest,

---

[103] The Bible and archaeology agree that, for some reason, the Sea Peoples did not occupy Sidon. It remained Canaanite. Later, when the Greeks came along, these northern Canaanites were called Phoenicians.

came outside and stood beside me, saying nothing. My men took the images and the ephod and came out.

"What are you doing?" the Levite finally asked. My men had told me about this shrine, so I said to the Levite, "Just be quiet. Say nothing. Come with us, and be our father and priest. Is it not better to be the priest of a whole clan and tribe than to be the priest of one household?" The Levite looked at the idols, now behind the shield wall, and at the rows of spears, and he smiled. You could tell that he saw wisdom in my question. So he came with us, and he personally carried the images and the ephod as we moved on north.

I had made the order of march such that a small forward guard led the way, followed by the mass of our people, and then our six hundred armed men. I stayed with the main troop, having a system of runners going back and forth to the front of the host.

As we left, we heard the alarm call on the ram's horn, and we closed ranks. Sure enough, just after we had filled our water jars at a spring, there came a rag-tag group of farmers, led by a man who was shouting at us to stop and waving some tool.

Partly because there was no real danger, and partly to show my men that I had courage even when they did not surround me, I walked back to the man and said, quietly so as not to stir up our hot-heads, "What is the matter with you, coming out after us and asking for a fight?"

The man yelled that we had taken his goods, all that he had. We had not taken all he had, of course, and I told him so. Had we searched his house, or the houses of his neighbors, and had we taken anything but those things in his shrine? and besides, the priest had consented to take them and go with us. The man was upset. I said to him, "Go back home. You see this army. Some of them are hot tempered. If you make a scene or seem to threaten me, they will fall upon you and your men, and go back and wipe out your families as well. You know that we are Danites, and that we have no concern for you of Ephraim. Go home quietly."

My men were fidgeting and balancing their spears as if to cast them, so the man went away. I walked back to the troop, snapped them to attention, and moved them out after the rest of the tribe. It was done.

The rest of our march north was uneventful. True to the report of the scouts, Laish was not prepared for us. We concentrated our forces and first took the main town, leveling it after we had killed its inhabitants. We remembered the command of the great general Joshua, to leave no survivors to trouble us[104]. We then systematically mopped up the surrounding towns and farms, clearing the entire valley for ourselves. There were survivors who fled to Sidon and to other places, but they did not concern us.

There was a high place in Laish, one that had served for worship from time before memory. It was made to order. We installed the Levite with his images and his ephod, and the two images. We made our headquarters camp around the high place. We named the city Dan to help establish our tribe. We did not rebuild the houses; tents were good enough for us, so we built a tent city. We did not need walls, because our warriors were strong.

The rest of our tribe scattered over the valley. I reserved one spot for myself and my family, a place where a great spring of fresh water flows out of a cliff[105]. It is cool in

---

[104] This massacre at Laish was pretty much the same as the killing of other Canaanites in the towns taken by the other tribes under Joshuah.

[105] The spring at Banias is one of the major sources of the Jordan River. Another source is a spring at Tell Dan. The Banias spring runs right out from under a cliff, and it has been the place of various shrines for millennia. I do not know whether the Danites made a shrine there, but their territory now included Banias, and they would

the summer there, and there is a grove of trees for shade. Although we generally lived in tents, even in our towns, I decided to make use of one of the buildings as my home. It is cooler to live in a roofed house than in a tent.

I must give some thought to building a shrine at the great spring. But that can wait. We have our high place at the town of Dan, and the shrine is within a built wall. The shrine itself, though small, is large enough to shelter the images and to store the ephod. The Levite lives in a large nearby tent, and he has been given one of our tribe's best young women to wife. May his clan increase!

We are settled. We worship the LORD[106]. We have enlarged the Land. May Joshua rest in peace!

---

have made use of the spring.

[106] Images and ephods or not, it is clear that the Danites and their Levite thought that they were worshipping the God of Israel. They were doing it wrong, but they evidently really thought that the images in some way helped them to worship the LORD.

ONE ANGRY LEVITE
Judges 19:1 - 21:25
*This man with no name set in motion a series of events
that nearly wiped out one of the twelve tribes. My bet is
that, in his rage, he wouldn't care.*

They should have all died. Every Benjamite, and every
Gibeahite especially. Gibeah is the root, and Benjamin
is the tree.

I bought my concubine legally. I paid her father in sheep
that I had purchased in his home town of Bethlehem
Judah. He was content. The woman was sixteen years
old, and she was content. She was no beauty, but I am
a man of broad tastes; I was content. So she came with
me to the hills of Ephraim, and lived with me.

But our green hills did not suit her. She was idle,
because I am a man with enough substance to have
household servants. All I asked of her was to warm my
bed and be pleasant. She was pleasant enough, until
she became restless. Then I was not enough, and she
strayed.

I beat her, but not severely. She promised to become
faithful, so there was no point in having either her or my
neighbor killed[107]. I only took compensation from my
neighbor. She was, after all, not married to me, and
hence there was no serious reflection on my honor. She
was my concubine, and concubines are not themselves
capable of honor or dishonor, nor of giving it.

She disappeared. There was no great secret of where
she would go. I waited for word, and sure enough, her
father sent the message to me that she had returned
home. Meanwhile, for four months my bed was cold,
and I bethought myself of my property.

---

[107] The penalty for adultery was death, but the woman here was
"only" a concubine.

When I got to Bethlehem that second time, I found her in the marketplace, and I determined that she had been lessoned by her father enough so that she saw me as a kind and caring master at least. She took me to her home, where her father greeted me warmly. He told me that he had made sure that Sarah's stay with him was not too comfortable. He and I liked each other, for all the difference in our standing. As for Sarah, she welcomed me with some enthusiasm, and I also found that I had quite a bit of affection for her. We all agreed to let bygones be bygones, and that Sarah would come back to Ephraim and be a good concubine. If she bore a man child, perhaps I would marry her. In fact, I liked her so well that I had already determined to make her more than a concubine, but of course I did not tell that to her or to her father. She would have to prove herself worthy.

Hospitality in Bethlehem was more than I had planned for. Sarah's father, as is customary, insisted that I stay three nights. That was well enough. On the fourth day, he prevailed on me to sit down and eat and drink, and before we knew it, the day was too far gone for me to depart. He insisted on refreshing me on the next day also, and I saw that day slipping away as well. I had important business back in the hill country, and I wanted to stop at the Sanctuary at Shiloh on the way, so when I saw that the day was nearly gone, I finally broke away from his hospitality and we departed, I and my servant and the concubine, with the servant leading her donkey.

It is not far from Bethlehem to Jebus Salem[108], and within the first couple of hours we were passing that city. We paused at the gushing spring below the city to refill our water bag, and my servant suggested that we spend the night there. But I did not want to sleep in the city of the heathen Jebusites, thinking that we could easily get to Gibeah beyond Jebus before full nightfall. I had counted on safety in a city of my fellow Israelites.

---

[108] Jerusalem - - remember?

Little did I know that my own countrymen, Israelites though they were of the tribe of Benjamin, would be worse than the heathen!

We did get to Gibeah before they closed the gate for the night. Gibeah was a surly city. Small though it is, the people seemed not to cluster together like they do at home or in Bethlehem. People looked at us and passed on, sometimes smiling without humor. They passed each other without greeting, and they went into their houses and shut the doors. No one talked to us, as we sat in the city square and waited for hospitality. I was uneasy, but not really afraid. We had supplies enough for ourselves and our donkeys, I am used to sleeping where I can, and surely the servant and the concubine could stand the night air.

An old man came in from the fields as the gates were shut, and told us that we could not spend the night in the square. He did not say why, and I interpreted his solicitude as that of a rare hospitable person in an inhospitable town, and I let him persuade us to enter his house. Once we were in, and the donkeys tied in the inner court, I noticed that his door was more sturdy than ours at home, and that it was equipped with a bar like that of a rich man's house, though he was by no means rich.

The man's wife and daughter saw to my concubine, and the old man himself served me and my servant with bread and wine.

Then the reason for the barred door became evident. There was a murmuring outside that grew, then a pounding on the door. Many men were out there, and they demanded what I can barely speak of. They wanted me -- me, a Levite! -- to be put out to them so that they could use me as one uses a woman. I can speak of such things now, because worse was to come.

The old man tried to reason with the men outside, and to remind them of the Law. They laughed. The laughter sticks in my memory like a camel-thorn burr. The laughter was coarse and it was clear that some of the men were drunk.

The old man tried to protect me. He offered them not only my concubine, but also his virgin daughter. This last was more than I could bear. For the men outside to take a virgin and destroy her life was almost as bad as their desire to take me. To cut the siege short, I put out my concubine, and we spent the night waiting to see if the offering was enough. We slept not at all. I was shocked at the wickedness of the men who had wanted me, a middle-aged man of no great attractiveness, and their openness about the whole evil enterprise. The sounds outside ebbed and flowed, and my concubine's wails quieted.

When morning came, the men were gone. The town was silent. I arose early so as to avoid contact with the townspeople. I resolved to get out as soon as the gates were opened. The town was cursed. I had had to turn my concubine over to the wicked men, and it was best to get away and deal with my guilt regarding her as well as I could. Now I definitely needed to get to the Sanctuary at Shiloh quickly, and make atonement.

And there, on the doorstep, lay my concubine. She had been stripped, and she lay face-down with her hands on the doorsill, not moving. She was now unclean, but I felt, as I have explained, an affection for her. I touched her and said, "Get up. Let us go." There was no answer. To compound the evil of the demand to use me as a woman, and the evil of misusing my concubine, the men had abused her so badly that she had died. How could they do this and still count themselves as Israelites? It was not to be borne.

I called down curses on the town, and I resolved to visit the iniquity of the place upon its head. The old man believed, and trembled. I told him to take his wife and daughter and leave the town within a week, promising him protection in Ephraim if he needed it. He said that he had relatives in Judah, and that he would be gone when the curse fell on Gibeah, because it was a heavy curse and I was enraged.

I put Sarah's dead body on the donkey and went out of the town gate at daybreak. Pushing the donkeys and my servant to make haste out of the cursed tribe of Benjamin, I made my way to my home territory in a forced march of one day, tearing my robe and shaking off the dust of Gibeah at the border of Benjamin just beyond Bethel.

Back in the hill country of Ephraim, I divided my concubine's body[109] and hired a dozen men with donkeys. I had a scribe write out the proclamation, and had the men commit it to heart also, then sent them on their ways. Each bore a part of my concubine's body, and the message: this is what the men of Gibeah have done. Then I went to Shiloh to be purified, and to atone for my guilt. The guilt of Gibeah could not be atoned by any sacrifice.

Then I waited at Mizpah to see what Israel would do. The unprecedented message and its awful tokens stirred up the people against Gibeah. Israel gathered to me at Mizpah, four hundred thousand men of war. They had me repeat the story, tearing their clothes and throwing dust into the air at the word of such vileness. They were ready to avenge the LORD upon Gibeah, and sent men

---

[109] This treatment of a dead body is contrary to all principles of Judaism. It would be enough to arouse the indignation of the whole nation, and the Levite wanted to arouse indignation. Of course, the people could have as easily turned against the Levite for his mutilation of a corpse, instead of turning against Gibeah. The whole action was horrifying.

to get provisions for a battle. The matter was now out of my hands[110]. Let the LORD judge.

But first, as was right, they sent to Benjamin, the tribe where the town of Gibeah was and the tribe that had not come out to Mizpah. "Deliver up the men of Gibeah who have done this thing, and we will be satisfied," they said to Benjamin. But Benjamin united behind Gibeah, unwilling to let other tribes come in and fall upon a town of their own. I stood back, with events out of my hands, and let the curse work before the LORD.

You know the story. Benjamin was defeated, although they inflicted heavy losses on the rest of Israel. The anger of Israel was great. After killing all but the six hundred Benjamite warriors who escaped, Israel went through the land of Benjamin, putting every living thing to the sword, until the curse was accomplished.

Then Israel repented of wiping out one of its tribes, and wept. But they had bound themselves with an oath. I went home justified. By a trick evasion of their oath, the other tribes permitted Benjamin to re-establish itself, but I would have left them destroyed if it had been up to me. I stayed at my home and my work, knowing that the Law had been fulfilled. And I was the one who saw to its fulfillment.

---

[110] The Bible does not tell us that the Levite took any part in the vengeance he had called down with his curse on Benjamin and Gibeah.